Last Cast

Bar and Grill

By Earl Morrogh

ISBN: 9798366901239

For Judye,
my faithful partner, great love of my life,
best friend, and fearless editor.

Keep some room in your heart for the unimaginable.

Mary Oliver

CHAPTER 1

I deeply long for the love of my life and best friend I have ever had—my wife, Yoku Kikuchi. We didn't have a chance to say goodbye. She was killed by a 12-year-old boy who lost control of his half-ton, over-powered, personal watercraft. I blame his parents. I am certain, like me, he will suffer from the tragedy for the rest of his life. Forensics estimated that he was going seventy when he ran up and over the hotel's sundeck where Yoku was sunbathing at the water's edge in the Florida Keys.

I was in Chicago nearing the end of a book tour. Dawn had arrived bright and clear. It was a spectacular spring morning. As I left my hotel to have breakfast at a favorite outdoor café near Lincoln Park, I received the call. Being a best-selling author has many benefits, but it is also exhausting. After weeks on the road signing books, I was particularly excited about being home with Yoku. Hanging up, I tumbled into a world of pain and darkness; for months afterward, suicide seemed like the only way out. There didn't seem to be any rhyme or reason as to when that dark desire would rise and eclipse the sun.

I'm not afraid of death; it's the dying part that undoes me. Being a creative type I have a hyperactive imagination. Knowing that most people who attempt suicide fail, it was easy to conceive of a thousand ways things could go horrifically wrong. So, coward that I am, I turned to alcohol. Eventually I became enamored with dive bars. My favorites probably began with high aspirations but through either folly or sheer neglect ended up falling into disrepair and ill repute. A proper dive bar has denizens rather than customers and a bathroom well below most standards of cleanliness. It's the kind of place that down-and-out, scuffed-up outcasts with no pride or shame gravitate to. No mystery why they come; they come for the same reasons I do—to medicate their misery, to silence painful secrets in their hearts, to tunnel toward oblivion.

Every dive I've loitered in smells of stale beer, rancid cigarette smoke, and soured sweat, but each also has its own distinctive fusion of odors. It was after midnight when I came upon The Last Cast Bar and Grill in Apalachicola, Florida. Tattered remains of duct tape clung to the word Grill on the hand-lettered sign, and I assumed they were no longer serving food. That was fine with me. I wasn't hungry. I noticed a familiar raw stink. A mountain of oyster shells was heaped up in the shadows alongside a nearby packing facility. I imagined that in the intense heat of mid-summer the stench would be powerful enough to drop the faint-hearted in their tracks. The bar was perched on the west bank of the Apalachicola River. Its sad, broken façade suggested to the fatalist in me that its name honored those who had given up hope for a better day after a last, fruitless cast into the difficult waters of life. I felt certain that, to a more optimistic soul, it was a reference to a fisherman's final, hopeful toss of the line before heading to shore for a cold one and to swap stories with friends.

But for the weathered sign illuminated by the blue-green light of a mercury vapor lamp nuking the nightscape, the Last Cast would have been easy to mistake for an abandoned warehouse. A few trucks parked out front provided the only clue that the place might be open. One was a sleek, late-model Ford; the others looked battered and blown by years of salt, sun, and heavy loads.

As I opened the door, my nose was greeted by the rotten-egg odor of hydrogen sulfide gas. Either the group of men huddled around the bar was collectively experiencing some serious gastrointestinal distress or marsh gas was blowing in from the nearby coastal wetlands. The bacterial breakdown of sulfates in organic matter in swamps and sewers can generate hydrogen sulfide gas, but none of the double-hung windows stretching shoulder-to-shoulder across the long wall facing the river was open. The place was closed tight—probably not marsh gas.

When I was with the *Miami Journal,* I covered a hydrogen sulfide story in the aftermath of Hurricane Andrew. Prolonged exposure to low levels of hydrogen sulfide gas can screw up coordination and breathing, and a demolition debris dump on the Gulf Coast of Florida was generating enough of the gas to be dangerous. Homeowners close to the dump complained and threatened to sue its owner. Turned out the culprit was hundreds of tons of wallboard damaged by flooding during Andrew. Gypsum is the primary ingredient in wallboard, and it produces volumes of hydrogen sulfide gas when it decomposes. Not unlike myself, the Last Cast did appear to be in a semi-advanced state of decomposition. Regardless, the odor was a temporary distraction. I was ready for a drink.

As I stepped toward the bar, it was immediately obvious that I'd disrupted some sort of meeting. Startled by my entrance, a dozen or so heads swiveled in unison toward me. No one held a drink or had one sitting on the bar. No one looked drunk. *Surely someone in a place like the Last Cast would be stewed this late in the evening,* I thought. They were all male except the bartender, a petite woman who snatched something—a large book or box—from the bar top, glanced briefly in my direction, turned away, and quickly retreated through a dark doorway at the far end of the bar into what I guessed was a kitchen or storeroom. She was younger-looking than her weather-beaten clientele who appeared to be oystermen. Her smooth, milky complexion and honey-colored hair stood in stark contrast to their deeply tanned and crevassed faces. Even the youngest among them looked dilapidated compared to her.

The men peered out from under the beaks of their faded baseball caps for a moment before acknowledging my presence. Shocks of coarse, sun-ravaged, wildly tangled hair haphazardly tucked under their caps framed their faces. After a few almost imperceptible nods, a flatly drawled "how you," a tug at the brim of a camouflage cap, and one raspy, "eening, sir," they broke away from the bar and headed to the door. I responded with a smile and a nod as I stepped aside to let them pass. Wearing t-shirts and work pants splattered gray with oyster shell and mud flecks, they slogged by in their predictable white rubber boots. This footwear appears to be an icon of the fishing industry worldwide—Croatian fishermen, Islanos crabbers, Vietnamese shrimpers, Apalachicola oystermen. I've never found a satisfying answer for why. Maybe it's nothing more notable than that they're cheap.

I've known a couple of Apalachicola oystermen in my time. Like the oyster itself, the oyster business is crusty and raw. This is particularly true on Apalachicola Bay where almost all the oysters are "pulled by hand," meaning they're carefully collected from the bottom with hand-operated, 12-foot tongs. Nothing about the work of oystering in the Bay has changed in 200 years except the motors that power the small, time-worn work boats. Years of raking, lifting, culling, and sacking oysters seven or eight hours a day make for a hard life. I can see these years in the tortured bodies of the older men as they file by—leathery skin, misshapen and hard hands, bent backs. Surprisingly, it is the old salts who are the first to say they don't mind working hard. Many come from families who have harvested the Bay for generations. They will tell you that if they can work the tongs and oysters cling to the Bay's bed, they will be out there earning a living, one 60-pound sack at a time. A sack of oysters was fetching close to $16 back then. Ten sacks would have been a rather good day. It's not a glamorous life, but oystermen are fiercely independent and enjoy both the freedom of being self-employed as well as the irrepressible natural beauty of their workplace, the Bay. The younger ones are looking for something else. They would rather do almost anything else but bust their asses, even if that means cleaning the expensive cars of the fat cats ensconced in gated communities on nearby St. George Island.

Miss Milk and Honey emerged from the back room as I sat myself down at the bar. She looked me straight in the eye, and said, "What's your pleasure, Mr. Nilsson?" I guess I shouldn't have been shocked that she knew who I was. She went on to say, "This is a nosey little town, and I must confess that I'm a huge fan of yours. Not easy to hide your comings and goings, you know? Besides, Shelly Wainwright's been passing around pictures she took of that fancy houseboat of yours. Boats are a big deal around here. One like the Starfish Enterprise, that's what folks are calling it, would make you a celebrity if you weren't one already."

Eye color is largely determined by the reflection of ambient light from the iris, but the bartender's irises were unusually large and aquamarine green with golden flecks and seemed to be lit from some brilliant interior source. They radiated intelligence. Her small talk and casual tone couldn't conceal the fact that she was assiduously studying me. When I finally found my voice, I replied, "And your name is?"

"Gamp," she said as she wiped her hands with a bar towel before extending one to me. She had a confident, welcoming grip. I've never been good at estimating a women's age, even though Yoku tried to teach me the tell-tale signs associated with the passage of time. I could never remember them. I thought maybe she was in her late 30s. "I'll be forty-one this September," she added.

"Pardon me," I said.

"You were trying to guess my age, right? I'd bet you're close to my father's age. Seventy?"

"Close. Sixty-five. Gamp? That's an uncommon first name."

"It's a nickname. Maybe you know who Sarah Gamp is? Character in a Dickens novel."

"Don't remember that one. I've heard gamp used as a slang word for an umbrella in Britain, though."

"*The Life and Adventures of Martin Chuzzlewit.* Sarah Gamp was an alcoholic midwife who did, as a matter of fact, always carry an old black umbrella. Thirsty?"

"Yes. Give me a double shot of your best tequila and a Red Stripe. You like Dickens?"

"Not really. My father did, though. He used to read to me when I was a kid. He loved the Sarah Gamp character. Any kids, Mr. Nilsson? Cuervo Gold okay?"

"Cuervo's fine. No kids of my own. My, uh, deceased wife was Japanese. She had two from a previous marriage. Born in Japan."

"Don't carry Red Stripe. Bud, Bud Lite, Miller, Miller Lite, Coors, Coors Lite. Close to the kids?"

"Bud. Nope. Raised by their father. Never left Japan."

"Read about your wife. I'm so sorry. Professor of Anthropology at University of Miami?"

"Yes, she was."

"Is that where you met her?"

"Nope. We met when I was a journalism student at San José State. She was up the road at Stanford and waited tables at a hole-in-the-wall Japanese restaurant in San José. I heard the food there was delicious and cheap. The rest, as they say, is history."

It was true that the restaurant, Tsugaru, was small and nondescript and that the food was delicious and inexpensive. It was also true that it was where Yoku earned rent money and where we met and fell in love. More than that, the restaurant was in San José's Japantown (Nihonmachi) where immigrant Japanese first settled in the Santa Clara Valley around 1890. By the early 20th century, Nihonmachi was a flourishing community where Japanese immigrants found cultural support, employment, goods, shelter, and a social life that was uniquely Japanese. Seventy plus years later, it was where Yoku, a child bride in an arranged marriage and a mother of two before she was 17, found refuge after divorcing her abusive husband and leaving Japan.

"Asking too many questions?"

"Getting close."

"Got it."

She was all business now, and her body moved with assembly-line efficiency as she fulfilled my order. Since it was almost 1:00 a.m., I guessed she was anxious to close. She started to place my tequila and beer on the bar but hesitated suddenly and put them off to the side. Reaching under the bartop, she pulled out a cleaning rag and quickly wiped off the area in front of me, erasing all traces of a dusting of fine white powder that I hadn't noticed until that moment. It was where whatever she'd snatched off the bartop had been sitting when I first arrived.

In the late 70s I covered a story about drug smuggling in South Florida Gulf Coast villages. Smuggling was a common practice among commercial fishermen who had fallen on hard times and were living hand-to-mouth. A night's work might net them $10,000—30,000 in today's dollars.

I knew Apalachicola's oysterman were suffering because there wasn't enough water coming down the Apalachicola River to maintain the unique balance of fresh and salt water in Apalachicola Bay that has made it one of the most productive marine ecosystems in North America. Less fresh water in the bay raises the salinity level allowing saltwater predators, such as the southern oyster drill and stone crab, to enter from the Gulf and raid the oyster beds. Record-breaking drought and increasing urban and agricultural demands on the waters of the Chattahoochee and Flint Rivers were the culprits. The Chattahoochee and Flint both originate in Georgia, and their confluence at the Georgia-Florida border forms the Apalachicola River.

It wouldn't have been a huge surprise to me if some of Apalachicola's oysterman were part-timing as cocaine cowboys for a South American drug cartel. That might explain Milk and Honey's late model truck. *Could be that she uses the Last Cast as a front for a drug smuggling operation. Too bad, she seems so wholesome,* I thought to myself as I reached for my wallet.

"On the house."

"You don't . . ."

"Not a problem. Just autograph my copy of *Water Weasels* next time you're in, Mr. Nilsson. Deal?"

"That's a deal. And please call me Eirik. I've never gotten used to being a mister or a sir. Makes me feel old, you know, and I don't care to be reminded that I *am* old."

Sometimes I think getting old is like the outgoing tide. When the water recedes, it exposes things that have been out of sight for so long you thought they no longer existed—regrets, resentments, hates, jealousies—an accumulation of emotional trash littering your life that you can no longer ignore. Old age is something I can deal with though, maybe even accept, and certainly write about.

Despair, on the other hand, has nearly rendered my heart and mind impotent. Forget about writing. I used to think I was suffering from writer's block and that at some point I would finally accept Yoku's death if I could just get my grief down on paper. It hadn't happened. My imagination tricked me into hearing her coming to bed or seeing her in the street. I invariably got out two cups as I brewed my morning tea. When preparing to travel to her grave site, I deluded myself into thinking I was simply going to visit the place where she *lived.* Only drinking gave me some occasional respite from the endless, jolting realizations that she is gone. Often, I ended up drunkenly casting about my memories of her like elephants do with the bones of their kin during their clumsy and ponderous funeral rites.

No accommodation or adjustment to losing Yuko that I tried gave me lasting comfort.

"We're only as old as we feel. Don't you think that's true...Eirik?" Gamp asked, snapping my attention out of its habitual dislocation.

"Of course...there's something to that. But surely you don't believe that an old body can feel young forever. You're *old* enough to understand that, right? "

"I'm just saying that our minds can be useful only if we use them. You know, the attitude thing."

Ah, yes, the attitude *thing*, I said. *Young people! Think they have it all figured out,* I thought to myself. With that, I picked up my shot of tequila, raised it in a toast, and said tauntingly, "And here's to attitude *adjustment*," downed it, and set the shot glass sharply on the bar. "A little more adjustment, uh, Gamp, please ma'am." She gave me a disapproving look. My fans invariably hold me to a higher standard than I hold myself.

"So, it *is* true," she said, smiling broadly.

"What's true?"

"The article in the *New York Times* a while back; the one that claimed you're a sot, a 'vinegary old sot,' if I remember correctly."

Who could forget *that* article? I was characterized as a "vinegary, embittered, and implacable old sot." I wondered if she'd also read the *Globe* article a couple of years before the *Times* article that held me up as "one of America's finest social commentators with a fondness for satiric wit" or, the *Post* article around the same time that stated I was nothing less than "a comic genius."

"Are you referring to that story about the incident with the TV reporter?"

"That's the one," she said as she delivered my second double-shot of tequila.

"You believe everything you read?"

"I didn't at the time, but here you are in *this* place at 1:00 a.m. and within five minutes of arriving you're already on your second double-shot of tequila and getting all snippy and shit." She rolled her shoulders up and added, "What would you think?"

The truth is that the *Times* was almost right about my drinking—it did border on being out of control. I drank a lot and frequently, but I didn't think I was anything like your typical alcoholic. Maybe that's a delusion that all addicts suffer. I was relatively healthy for a 65-year-old and my energy levels were high each morning. I did take a nap every afternoon, but I did that long before my life went to hell. My diet sucked but my appetite was good. I was rational most of the time. There was a lot to be pissed off about back then, and I think that explained why I got angry so often—that and the fact that I wasn't as patient as I used to be. Old people get grumpy. I wasn't numb like many addicts, at least no more than any other man who was emotionally miseducated as a boy. Regardless, I didn't end up being the tough, make-my-day silent type. I felt more deeply than any other time of my life—sometimes more than I really cared to. Nothing in my life prepared me for what felt like an irreparably broken heart.

"Mr. Nilsson? Eirik? Are you okay? I'm sorry if. . .me and my big mouth. . ."

Gamp's face was filled with sincere concern as she spoke. I guess I had turned away from her during my reverie. She was now on my side of the bar standing directly in front of me.

"Don't worry, dear. You've done nothing to offend me. I'll be fine. Really, I'm just feeling very tired all of a sudden. I should go."

"You aren't getting out on the river at this time of night, are you? There's some nasty weather blowing in from the Gulf. There's a room. . .You're welcome . . ."

"I'm staying at the Half Shell. I walked. Thank you for your concern, though. What do I owe you?"

"We made a deal, remember?"

“Oh, yes, sign your copy of *Water Weasels* next time I’m in town. Will do. I downed my second shot of tequila and said, ‘Good night, sweetheart. It was a pleasure meeting you.”

“Good night, Eirik, please come back soon.”

CHAPTER 2

Offering eight tiny rooms, the Half Shell Motel was tucked under the great expanse of an ancient live oak tree. Although the exterior looked as weather-beaten as oystermen, the rooms were clean and comfortable. I stayed at the Half Shell when coming off the river and into town to do my weekly food and booze shopping. Long strands of Spanish moss were blowing like tattered storm flags from the oak's arms by the time I got back to my room. I undressed, got into bed and waited for the tequila's warm waves to lull me into sleep. Instead, I lay there reconstructing the sequence of events that led to my becoming an "old sot."

Charles Shorter, my literary agent, thinks the bad press *and* diminished book sales began about a year after Yuko died, when I was hawking *Water Weasels* at one of New York's largest bookstores. It was there I got into a shouting match with a twenty-something reporter from Celeb-TV sporting one of those Japanese spikey, anime-inspired hair styles. He no doubt thought he was very cool, but I thought he resembled a terrified blowfish with pouty, oversized, Mick Jagger lips. He'd pissed me off because of the way he and his equally age-deficient cameraman pushed and shoved their way through a crowd of fans (most in their sixties and seventies) waiting for me to sign their copies of *Weasels*. When the blowfish began peppering me with questions about a recent DUI, I "suggested" to the rude little bastard he should shut up or I would rip his colossal lips off!

He retaliated with a string of obscenities and my normally serene fans jumped him, cursing and pummeling him with whatever was in their hands, mostly purses, umbrellas, and copies of my book. When his camera guy tried to pull him off the floor and save him from the wrath of dozens of temporarily insane senior citizens—who I suspect were collectively exorcising their irritation with the fatuousness of youth-culture in general—the camera guy, and his $40,000 hi-def camera were drawn down into the vortex of the geriatric mosh pit while the camera continued to roll. Within hours the altercation was uploaded to YouTube, and before day's end the video clip, now known by tens of thousands around the world as "Old People Kick Ass," was picked up by the major news networks.

I found the whole scene fascinating from a purely socio-media point of view *and* deeply entertaining—all those red-faced white-hairs looked like they *were* getting off kicking that young fart's butt. My agent, on the other hand, considered the seemingly endless primetime video stream featuring my outburst, and deranged-looking seniors flailing away at the boy-fish, to signify nothing less than the end of my and, I guess more than likely, his career. Having squirreled away all the cash I would ever need years ago, I couldn't have cared less.

My theory for the steady decline in book sales was that my readers were dying off. In fact, the rate at which sales were declining was in perfect sync with the rising age-specific mortality rate of early-born boomers. Apparently, thousands of my fans who were born in the mid-forties are dropping like pot-bellied flies. They've porked themselves into an epidemic of heart and pulmonary diseases, Type 2 diabetes, colon cancer, sleep apnea, and non-alcoholic liver disease. Charles thought this was pure Freakonomics bullshit and I should check myself into Betty Ford, dry out, get some grief counseling, start using a little "anti-aging" product, and get back to writing. You would think with a Pulitzer for investigative reporting, eight best-selling novels, and millions of copies of my books out there, he wouldn't want me to mess with a formula that's been a cash cow for his agency for almost thirty years. He charged that my journalistic style and weird over-the-top characters turned off younger readers and they were also tired of being beaten over the head with tales about Florida's environmental destruction, dumb blondes, and corrupt politicians. "Comic-crime is so last millennium," he said.

Maybe he was right, but I really didn't give a shit about the opinion of an entire generation that uses its thumbs to dial a phone or "text" on a keyboard the size of a credit card or shares naked pictures of themselves and all the intimate details of a recent hookup—who, how big, how long, how good—with *hundreds* of their "friends." De Quervain's Tendinosis affects tendons on the thumb side of the wrist and is caused by chronic overuse. "Overuse" is a euphemism for addiction, and DQT cases were increasing so rapidly that the medical community characterized the problem as a crisis. An early symptom of DQT is "numb thumb."

Numb Thumbs also think aging is the worst possible thing that can happen to them, like it is a disease. I believe this is the result of the relentless barrage of age-loathing propaganda aimed at them. No wonder the anti-aging marketers are having a field day exploiting our age-phobic culture and raking in billions. Under the illusion of immortality, they're also masking their fears with optimism and convincing themselves that thinking about the fragility of life and the inevitability of death is a betrayal of their "spiritual" roots. I was certain it wouldn't be long before young adults were desperately mainlining essence of snail saliva, snorting freeze-dried sheep placenta, or gorging on South Korean Penis Fish (a marine worm) in a vain attempt to avoid facing life's inevitable conclusion.

Regardless, I couldn't imagine anyone of any age suffering through what I was experiencing without feeling bitter or resorting to some form of escapism. As devastating as losing Yuko was, it wasn't her tragic death alone that drove me to drink. Over the better part of my adult life, despite my efforts and the efforts of hundreds of other concerned individuals and various local environmental groups, I watched Southwest Florida's burgeoning population, and all that comes with unrestrained land and resort development, devastate the Alligator Creek Estuarine Sanctuary. At first, due to the degradation of habitat critical for fish spawning and incubation, once-abundant numbers of grouper, grunt and snapper disappeared. Unabated dredging, draining, bulldozing, and paving; pollution; sewage discharges; and the toxic grime generated by the daily activities of hundreds of thousands of human beings led to the death of the Sanctuary's coastal marshes and the subsequent disappearance of the wildlife dependent upon it.

As a boy, I grew up exploring the Alligator's fragile, mysterious wetlands. Yoku said that even before getting to know me she divined that water ran deep in my soul. Along with the death of this irreplaceable oasis for wildlife, and another priceless human resource, part of me also died. When will we finally realize that there is no distinction between the fate of the natural world and people? Still, although down, I was not out.

Search engines and Baby Pandas would finally crush my spirit. Six rounds of layoffs at the *Miami Journal* had left me as the oldest, more experienced reporter among a handful of newbies. Unable to afford investigative reporters, fat staffs, or experienced journalists with higher salaries, newspapers all over the country were cutting deep to keep up their profit margins. This was true at the *Journal,* so much so that we were struggling to serve our communities. I'm not talking about just investigative reporting. Reporters were being pushed to keep up blogs as well as cover multiple beats.

We were all grieving for the way things were just a couple of years earlier. There was a heaviness in the newsroom I felt each morning as soon as I arrived at my desk. So many stories we were publishing came straight from press releases and didn't look beneath the surface for the story behind the story. Forget following a lead that required a plane ticket or even the expense of road mileage. I was also grieving for my colleagues who had been forced to leave the business. Cutting corners was cutting away at the heart of what motivates journalists. The profession of journalism as I knew it was dying. More and more, we began to look and operate like the tabloids.

The newsroom was being pressured to utilize online tools to research key words most frequently used by people searching on the various topics each of us wrote about. Knowing search engines scan the title, headline, and the first hundred words or so of news articles, the idea was that these key words could then be strategically placed in our stories, thereby raising the probability our articles would appear at the top of reader's search results. It wasn't difficult to predict this concept would soon drive editorial policy and before long stories would be selected, written, and promoted with the value of key words in mind. Such a strategy would ultimately lead to stupid headlines receiving undue prominence—front page headlines like the Tribune's infamous "Baby Pandas!"

We all knew what we were being asked to do was essentially marketing. For as long as I had been in the business, journalists took pride in their ignorance of anything to do with advertising, marketing and sales. Pushed to its logical conclusion, I could see that a search engine optimization editorial policy would combine editorial and advertising responsibilities in a single person—the journalist. The ethical and professional issues were too profound for me to ignore. I wasn't going to cross that line. I had had it. Having heard too many funeral bells, I abandoned the rules and rituals by which I kept my life in order and my impulsive tendencies in check. I quit the *Journal,* sold everything, hit the road, and hit the bottle.

CHAPTER 3

There are at least twenty-five navigable freshwater streams in Florida's Big Bend. Add to that, two hundred miles of Gulf coastline; hundreds of tidal and estuarine rivers, creeks, sloughs, bayous and bays; and four lakes over a thousand acres, and you have a water lover's paradise. When Yoku and I visited the area together for the first time, she noted that she'd never seen me happier or more relaxed and encouraged me to think about moving. I knew what she was saying was true, but journalism was a ride that I was not ready to get off at the time. As often as I'd been disappointed in my years at the *Journal,* I still lived for the opportunity to do something worthwhile—to change the world. Now with Yoku *and* my idealism dead, I found myself gravitating toward water once again; this time, I wanted to drown myself in solitude and the solace of tequila.

The Big Bend is wilderness compared to South Florida and unmatched in the Eastern United States for abundance, diversity, and untouched natural beauty. Unlike peninsular Florida, the area is sparsely populated and suffers relatively few heavy tourist infestations. Also known as

Middle Florida, the Bend includes the ten counties lying between Florida's two largest rivers, the Apalachicola to the west and the Suwannee to the east. All of it is less than two hours' driving distance from Tallahassee, the capital and the region's main population center, two hundred miles from anywhere else and surrounded by swamps, forests, and wildlife sanctuaries.

Sitting at the mouth of the Apalachicola River, the old port town of Apalachicola appealed to me too. It hadn't yet suffered the fate of so many Florida coastal villages destroyed by unregulated development and, except for a few up-scale shops and restaurants, was essentially still a fishing town. Refrigerated panel trucks rolled through loaded with crabs and flounder. Pickups rounded corners piled high with burlap sacks filled with oysters. A few shrimp boats, with their nets and gear hanging from high masts, still docked downtown. I also liked the way the word Apalachicola looked on paper and the little dance my tongue did when sounding it out. "Apalachicola" is reportedly a combination of Hitchiti Indian words: "apalahchi" meaning "on the other side," and "okli," meaning "people." Originally, it probably meant "people on the other side of the river." Many inhabitants of Apalachicola, however, choose to translate the name of their town as "land of the friendly people."

However friendly its people or charming a place it might be, I decided I wanted to appreciate it from afar. In my experience, people from small towns are often provincial, incurious, and small-minded, even, perhaps especially, when they don't think they are. Yoku chastised me more than once for this "snobbish" attitude saying that small towns are filled with people who have a deep connectedness to place, to people, and to their pasts—something that was being swept away throughout the country by the storm surge of commercial culture. She was right, of course, but I grew up in a small town and knew that that kind of connectedness can also breed parochialism and an attitude of suspicion toward the new or different—toward the outsider. I found the perfect spot ten miles up the river to park The Essex. Reachable only by water or a full day's hike through swampy terrain, it was a place so out of the way that only a true friend, or determined enemy, would make the effort to visit me. Living in seclusion along the banks of the Apalachicola River was precisely where an old sot like me needed to be.

Everything was shrouded in a thick morning mist when I left the Half Shell and headed downtown to Bakin' and Eggs for breakfast. As I walked through Lafayette Park, I admired the large octagon-shaped gazebo set at the center of the park overlooking Apalachicola Bay. The eight-sided gazebo was popularized by the Victorians who viewed the octagon as a symbol of graceful living. Apalachicola's roots date back to the early 1800s when it flourished as a port for the cotton trade between New England and Europe, but life in Apalachicola was not always graceful. Nearby in the Chestnut Street Cemetery, which dates to 1831, there are headstones of Confederate soldiers and sailors who defended Apalachicola from a Union blockade in the Civil War as well as those of scores of townspeople and visitors who died decades before the war from the "fevers." One of Apalachicola's most famous residents, Dr. John Gorrie, didn't discover in his lifetime the source of the yellow fever epidemics that beset the town each summer, but his research into a cure did lead him to invent a machine for making artificial ice. It was not until the 1880's that it was discovered that malaria is caused by infection with protozoan parasites transmitted by female Anopheles mosquitoes.

At the time, the theory that bad air caused diseases was a prevalent hypothesis. Malaria, Italian for bad air (mal-aria), and yellow fever prevailed in hot, low-lying, tropical and sub-tropical regions where there was high humidity and rapid decomposition of vegetation. Noxious effluvium or poisonous marsh gas was thought to be the cause. The "putrid" winds from marshy lowlands were regarded as deadly, especially at night. Based on this theory, Gorrie urged draining the swamps and the cooling of sickrooms. For this he used a basin filled with ice and suspended it from the ceiling. Cool air, being heavier, flowed down across the patient and through openings near the floor. Since ice had to be shipped by boat from the northern lakes, Gorrie experimented with making artificial ice. He succeeded and was granted a patent for his ice machine. He then sought to raise money to manufacture his machine, but the venture failed when his financial partner died.

Humiliated by criticism, financially ruined, and his health broken, Gorrie, according to some accounts, died in seclusion on June 29, 1855.

Along my route, brilliant rays of sunshine burned through the mist and reflected off dewdrops, bejeweling the leaves of grand old azalea and camellia bushes fronting meticulously restored Victorian homes. Mourning doves were singing muted background vocals to the bright chatter of chickadees, robins, and cardinals. As I strolled along, I intersected a stream of citrusy, delicate fragrance that I guessed was sent flowing through the cool, moist December morning air and across my path by the blossoms of an unseen witch-hazel shrub. *The splendid subtleties of a small historic southern town can even inspire the imagination of the living dead*, I thought to myself as I neared the Bakin'. It had been years since I felt anything as light as the breath of inspiration.

Some would call it contrived. I think a better single-word description of the Bakin' is quirky. Regardless of what anyone else thought, I liked the big sturdy wooden tables, the communal benches, mismatched chairs, cheery yellow paint job, bizarre assortment of flea market dishes and dishware glued to the walls, and the old floor-to-ceiling department store windows that allowed natural light to flood the place. Despite its breeziness, it was also cozy and was a good place to nurse a hangover and hot cup of tea—over fifty varieties of black, green, and herbal infusions served by the pot. I guess I liked the

Bakin' for breakfast as much as I eventually came to like the Last Cast for drinking. The creatively titled dishes on the menu were over-the-top cute and annoyed me some. Maybe if you're in a good mood they're funny. But the food was fresh and there was an eclectic assortment of sweet and savory fare offered. I usually opted for an apricot and dark chocolate scone with strawberry butter and chipotle hollandaise eggs.

After settling down at a table in a far corner and ordering, I realized I hadn't turned on my cell phone since turning off the damned thing over 24 hours earlier. I think the world and I are growing farther apart. Everyone is plugged into cyberspace and unplugged from the real world around them. It's alarming to me that masses of people are constantly glued to their "smart" phones, endlessly texting, talking, and whatever the hell else they do.

Charles had been harassing me about getting started on my next book and was calling at odd hours. I've never liked the idea of being accessible by phone anywhere at any time, but living on The Essex and not having a land line necessitated that I own a cell. I turned it on as my cup of Keemun tea arrived. I love Keemun's rich, smoky flavor and distinctive aroma. Charles had left no less than three voicemail messages. I debated for a moment whether to first enjoy my tea or playback his messages. I listened to the most recent message. "Madoff's been arrested! Call me!" he screeched.

I began investing small amounts with Bernard Madoff through a trusted friend and attorney whose family had been his clients for 20 years. I assumed my money was safe because he knew much wealthier people who were also longtime investors. "I'm not a financier, I'm a writer. I don't know anything about hedge funds," I said to him. He said to trust him. "Bernie's brilliant. He's invented this 'algorithmic technology' that no one else has," he said. I took comfort that these people, who had a lot more money sense than I, saw fit to invest with Madoff. After several years of steady earnings, I decided to place all my holdings I'd earned from book royalties and speaking fees. I'd met Bernie by this time, and on one occasion, he took me aside and assured me that he would "take care of me." I consider myself to be a good judge of character, and I found him to be a genuinely warm and charming man. I eventually came to consider him a friend. His assurances, plus consistent and spectacular earnings, eventually led me to invest all the cash from the sale of my South Florida properties. I was into Bernie hook, line, and sinker.

Rumor had it, among a few Madoff investors I knew, that our investments might be recoverable. However, it could take the trustee assigned by the court to oversee the Madoff recovery initiative years to settle our claims. There was also talk that individual cash advances of up to $500,000 might be made quickly if one was deemed eligible. Regardless, we were all feeling homicidal.

Losing money because of poor judgment made me feel stupid; losing it as a victim of a con made me feel used and stupid. Being conned by someone I'd come to trust set my emotions on fire, and vengeful fantasies raged uncontrolled in my imagination. The most prevalent reason for torture among pirates was to extract the whereabouts of their victim's valuables. One of the fastest and most effective tortures they used was called "woolding" named after the term used to describe the binding of cords around a mast. It required only a short length of rope positioned around the victim's head. The ends of the rope were secured onto a length of wood that would be continually twisted in a clockwise motion, thereby pulling the cord tighter and tighter against the victim's temples until they could no longer suffer the pain and pressure and gave up their secrets.

On the first night after getting the shocking news, I had a cartoonish-like dream in which I woolded the sleazy bastard to the point where he gave me all the information I needed to get my money back. I continued tightening the rope until the immense pressure eventually caused his eyeballs to pop out of his head and roll around on the salon floor of The Essex like marbles, ala Wile E. Coyote, the Looney Tunes cartoon character. I am no oneirologist, but I later thought it was likely that this scene in my dream drew upon the Chuck Jones autobiography that I'd read a few years earlier. Jones was the animation director who created a series of characters for Warner Brothers, including Wile E. based on the coyote in Mark

Twain's *Roughing It.* Twain described the coyote as "a long, slim, sick, and sorry-looking skeleton" that is "a living breathing allegory of Want. He is *always* hungry." Maybe it was this insatiable characteristic of the coyote as described by Twain that my subconscious linked to Madoff and mashed up with Chuck Jones' Wil E. Coyote.

My dream world has always been influenced by obvious factors in my life—the associations between what's going on in my day-to-day with what's happening in my dreams at night are almost always direct and simple. But nightmares are a different story. I worry about nightmares because I think what they reveal is less obvious—fears, guilt, anger, or unresolved emotionally toxic crap that I don't want to face and have managed to push out of my waking mind into my subconscious. After Yuko's death I experienced frequently occurring and graphic dreams that were filled with hatred and cruelty. My reasoning at the time was that I wasn't going to demean myself by caving into my baser instincts and consequently stuffed my feelings. The dreams relented only after spending endless hours beating the crap out of a perfectly innocent punching bag at a local martial arts gym and I finally exhausted my anger towards Yoku's youthful killer and his parents.

I had over $6,000,000 under management in Bernard Madoff Investment Securities. Then someone flipped a switch, and it was erased in an instance. The financial piers supporting a lifetime of accumulated wealth were all gone. I needed to get some cash flowing to be able to pay the bills in between my shrinking royalty checks. Learning to live without the financial freedoms I had enjoyed for so many years was going to be challenging. I really didn't know what in the hell I had left to live for. I guess having "survived" the loss of Yoku—whose love and companionship were priceless—I was not ready to give up on life over losing a few million bucks. She would have been ashamed of me for doing so.

CHAPTER 4

After a week of wallowing in equal measures of self-pity and alcohol, I surfaced. A cold front had moved into the basin. I watched mist rising on the river as its relatively warm waters met the cooler, drier air. Sitting out on the aft deck of The Essex drinking my morning tea, two stray clouds, fluffy and fat like enormous floating house cats, kept me company. A northwest breeze warned me that even colder air was on the way. I mused that the flow of a river is often used in literature as a metaphor to connote a timeless and unseen dimension or, to portend an unknown future.

Despite the natural beauty that surrounded me, I could come up with only one river metaphor to describe my life—I was up Shit Creek without a paddle. I considered that an Australian variation might be more applicable—Up Shit Creek without a paddle in a barbed wire canoe. The author making this claim broke down the meaning of the expression something like this: Up Shit Creek means you are in a very unfortunate situation, indeed. Not only are you navigating a fast-flowing, unforgiving waterway, the name of the god-forsaken stream is Shit Creek. In the grand Australian tradition of unimaginative naming conventions (see Shark Bay or the Grand Sandy Desert), Shit Creek is a little too eponymous to be anything other than a nightmare location. Without a paddle is almost self-evident; you have nothing with which to struggle hopelessly but bravely against the current. Being up Shit Creek, with the only way to attempt a change of direction being with some part of your body, you're not going to escape unscathed should you attempt to modify the speed and direction of your descent into hell. You don't have, in effect, even a bad plan for deliverance. In a barbed wire canoe describes not only the utter foolishness of your situation but also exactly how ill-prepared you were and how uncomfortable you are at the time. A more contemporary American variation I recently heard was a near perfect fit: Up Shit Creek without a paddle and the repo men are waiting on the shore for the boat.

Fortunately, I owned The Essex outright but until I went to work, and more money was flowing in, I could no longer afford the luxury of living in such splendid isolation. After my tea I would be moving her downstream to Apalachicola. I was hoping to pick up some freelance journalism work, while I worked on my next book and avoid selling her. *Curse you Madoff, you crook-pated moldwarp,* I thought to myself. Having come across an Elizabethan insult generator on the Web, I'd decided that if I was going to hate the fobbing, fen-sucked, clotpole, I might as well have some fun doing it. I'd jotted down a dozen or so insults and tossed then into a file folder thinking I'd work them into a future story. Cursing is a lost art. The ultimate insult has been reduced to, "fuck you muthafucka," or, "you suck, muthafucka." I was looking forward to hurling a devastating "get off the planet you pribbling, ill-nurtured, maggot-pie" the next time some pathologically smartphone-addicted, thumb-texting, muthafucka ran me off the road.

Bernie Madoff's face went flitting through my mind. Before it triggered another debilitating spasm of hate, my attention was drawn outward by two does peacefully grazing in a grassy clearing on the opposite bank of the river. Although they were standing in an island of shade, I could see their ears twitching and shifting, scrutinizing each new sound emanating from river, sky, and forest. For me, watching animals in the wild fills some larger, less purposeful appetite in much the same way that reading poetry does, or listening to music. The scene called to mind a poem, *The Deer,* by Mary Oliver, that coincidentally was inspired by two does grazing.

The Deer

You never know.
The body of night opens
like a river, it drifts upward like white smoke,

like so many wrappings of mist.
And on the hillside two deer are walking along
just as though this wasn't

the owned, tilled earth of today
but the past.
I did not see them the next day, or the next,

but in my mind's eye -
there they are, in the long grass,
like two sisters.

This is the earnest work. Each of us is given
only so many mornings to do it -
to look around and love

the oily fur of our lives,
the hoof and the grass-stained muzzle.
Days I don't do this

I feel the terror of idleness,
like a red thirst.
Death isn't just an idea.

When we die the body breaks open
like a river;
the old body goes on, climbing the hill.

I found the stanzas about each of us being given only so many mornings to "look around and love the oily fur of our lives, the hoof and the grass-stained muzzle," especially poignant since losing Yuko. And the notion that my body will break down to circulate "like a river" and become a part of some other life, some different beauty, was a comforting concept for me. Yuko loved that line too. However, I still did not get, "the old body goes on, climbing the hill." Was she referring to the collective old body—humanity? That would make sense. I should have asked her when I had the opportunity, but my ego wouldn't let me take the risk of appearing to be a dumbass in the presence of a master.

Years before, in Middlebury, Vermont, I stood at the back of a chapel on the campus of a small liberal arts college and listened to Mary Oliver read from a recent work. The old, unornamented, rectangular, wood building didn't have a steeple and was diminutive in scale and character. Styled like many Quaker meeting houses built in the mid-nineteenth century, the architecture was meant to embody the ideals of simplicity, plainness, and equality. It was a place where believers could go and feel the presence of God without a whole lot of hoopla—unpretentious, like the poetess herself.

What struck me most about seeing her live for the first time was not the small, energetic woman in a colorful woolen cap reading some of the best nature poems of our time; it was her audience. The thoughtful-looking eccentrics in the rows ahead of me–most gone salt-and-pepper grey–received Oliver like a goddess. They were all so eager to be entertained and moved–laughing at the cleverness, sighing at the tenderness, lapping up each carefully crafted word, and hungering for more. Her poetry, written with a sure touch and a simple elegance, inspired me.

As I prepared to cast off from the banks of my river sanctuary and head downstream, I wondered where I was going to find the motivation to resume the onerous and humdrum task of making ends meet. It had been thirty years since my first best-seller ended my struggle to earn a decent living as a wordsmith. I was going to have to fall back on journalism while I worked on completing my next novel. *Dam you Bernie Madoff, you gleeking, fly-bitten, canker-blossom!* But it was the opinion of an old colleague from the *Journal* that earning a buck as a journalist, even with my credentials, wasn't going to be easy. He warned me that in the years following my departure, journalists around the country had been laid off in droves. I told him that that didn't make any sense. "You can't feed a 24-hour news cycle with fewer journalists," I said. He replied that that would be true if the news outlets were interested in the truth anymore. "The era of the unbiased voice is over. It is all about winning. Everything is spun. It's all propaganda now," he said, "reporters and producers have been replaced with political operatives and amateur ideologues!"

I guess I had seen it coming. It started with the fragmentation of the news on the Internet and cable television. People began choosing to listen exclusively to their side of the story. Bloggers and TV hosts began preaching only to the choir, reinforcing their convictions. Consumers of such self-validating "news" become even more entrenched in their prejudices and increasingly hostile to those who disagree with them.

In politics, I can see this process leading to extremism. As hardliners gain power within a group or party, they drive out moderates; what remains of the group is even more extreme, which drives out even more moderates; and so on. A party starts out complaining that taxes are too high; after a while it begins claiming that climate change is a giant hoax. Next thing you know, the lunatics on the extreme right will end up believing something as far-fetched as that all Democrats are Satanist pedophiles. Surely, I thought, someone still values solid investigative reporting. I wasn't willing to accept that victory had become more important in American life than truth.

I turned over The Essex's engine. It coughed loudly and frightened the grazing deer before it started and settled into a low, rolling idle. As I powered up and steered into the main channel of the river, they bounded toward the forest understory with brilliant white tails held high and flashing amid the dark shadows before they disappeared. As I turned my attention downstream, I saw, or at least I think I saw—it all happened so quickly—what appeared to be a bow hunter squatting in low brush at the river's edge. When I looked back, he was gone. I assumed he had been stalking the grazing deer and felt badly that I had disrupted his hunt. I think hunters generally have an unfair advantage. The kill ratio at a couple of hundred feet with a semi-automatic weapon and scope is virtually 100 percent. The animal, no matter how well-adapted to escape natural predation, has no way to escape death once in the cross hairs of a scope mounted on a rifle. Bow hunters, especially those who stalk their game, are a different story. They must be highly skilled and have a thorough knowledge of deer behavior to even be able to get close. I thought this guy must have been exceptionally good. Probably born and raised in the basin and like most locals had been hunting since he was a child. The only details I remembered about him were that he wasn't wearing a hat and his long, jet-black ponytail. Guess that stood out because the rest of his body was covered in camouflage-patterned clothing.

I wasn't in any rush to reach Apalachicola, but Gamp had offered me mooring in a slip adjacent to the Last Cast that a relative once used to run a charter fishing rig out of. She was going to meet me there to help me hookup The Essex to water and electricity. I was deeply appreciative of the offer and didn't want to keep her waiting. She was charging me practically nothing, but more importantly, being the only vessel docking there, I wouldn't be sandwiched between other boats as I would be at a public marina. The Last Cast would also serve as a visual barrier between The Essex and the steady stream of foot and automobile traffic on the riverfront's main artery, Water Street. Privacy is important to me. Living in a city or village of any size, no matter how exciting or charming, it doesn't take long before my claustrophobia flares and I feel as if I'm suffocating. Hopefully, on the weekends I'd be able to justify the added expense of traveling upriver to escape the daily rattle of Apalachicola. Unfortunately, the "Starfish Enterprise" burned fuel like the Starship Enterprise.

I would have preferred to sneak into town at dusk or dawn. I wasn't comfortable knowing that photographs of The Essex had already been passed around. My own celebrity was enough for me to deal with, but I could easily disguise myself. I might as well be piloting a 40-foot billboard advertising my presence. I was hoping that at midday on a weekend most everyone would be at home surfing lifestyle TV programs (each selling the promise of an endlessly improvable self, or home, or yard, or chicken salad), diving for the *unbiased* truth in the murky waters of the blogoshere or drowning themselves in the bottomless inanity of social networking. And should they be on the riverfront as I cruised past, I figured they'd be indoors hell bent on mindfully eating their way to perfection, heaven, or enlightenment in the upscale eateries that had recently invaded what had once been the bastion of the town's old-style diners (whose patrons routinely kept separate their relationship to the divine and food). To my disappointment, as I approached the small park and river walk bordering downtown, I could see that a platform had been set up. Scores of people were gathered around it. I was still too far away to read a banner spanning its width. It looked like one word. The first letter was an F. Another hundred feet down river and the entire word came into focus—FLOW. Having captured national headlines numerous times for being charged with acts of ecotage in the northwest, FLOW was familiar to me.

FLOW is an acronym that stands for the Fight to Liberate Obstructed Waterways. Reported to be a branch of the radical environmentalism group the Earth Liberation Militia (ELM). FLOW, like ELM, is infamous for using "direct action" to forward its political goals—direct action being a euphemism for either blowing stuff up or burning it down. Another couple of hundred feet and I was close enough to catch bits of what was coming through the public-address system. The hairy, agitated figure on stage, right arm raised and fist pumping the air, shouted, "The time has come for us to make up our minds about what is more important: the planet and the health of its people or the profits of those who destroy it!" Until that moment, I was not aware that FLOW had extended its reach to Florida or even the southeast. I suspected that this rally had something to do with the water war that had been going on between Alabama, Georgia, and Florida for twenty years without resolution. As if on cue, the speaker confirmed my suspicions with, "Greed is destroying the Apalachicola River and Bay! Let the river run free! Dump the dams! Dump the dams! Dump the dams!

If you used proximity to the stage as a measurement of support for FLOW, the 80 or 90 people right up against the stage would be 100% committed, and the dozen or so individuals 50 feet from the stage would be highly interested but not sold. One hundred feet back was a small group of 5 to 6 people who were obviously anti-FLOW—arms braced across their chests and disapproving scowls on their faces. Then, across Water Street on the steps of the old Cotton Exchange building, there was Gamp standing next to a tall, striking, silver-haired woman.

When Gamp looked in my direction, I waved. She waved back and then gestured toward the Last Cast before hugging her companion and heading down Water Street. I responded with a nod of my head. Before I broke my gaze away from the beautiful woman, I noticed a familiar figure. Someone from my past. He caught my attention because, as soon as Gamp walked away, he stepped out from one of the shops in the Exchange and seemed to be following her. I was certain he was a Bureau of Alcohol, Tobacco, Firearms, and Explosives (ATF) agent I'd met when I was investigating the Cali drug cartel in Miami. His body type was distinctive—a small head perched on top of a long neck extending from a pear-shaped torso resting atop two thin legs. As he walked, his head and neck swayed slightly; perfectly synchronized with the gentle rolling of his hips—goose-like. It could be no one other than Gary "Goose" Coot. *Why was he tailing Gamp*, I wondered. *Oh god, all I need now is to get entangled in a drug-smuggling investigation. Got to talk to Goose.*

CHAPTER 5

Unable to sleep, I sat out on the aft deck of the Essex. Accustomed to the rich darkness of upper-river nights my body had mistaken semi-darkness for dawn, and I awoke prematurely. I was saddened that even in a town as small Apalachicola, light pollution rendered the midnight sky gray and devoid of stars. I found it difficult to imagine that night on Earth was once so dark, Venus shone bright enough to cast shadows. Thanks to Bernie Madoff (the irony of a guy who made off with billions being named Madoff), I was losing yet another valued freedom and would be forced to cover the windows of my stateroom with "blackout curtains" to get a decent night's sleep. Used to be that blackout curtains kept artificial light *in.* During WWII, the glow from coastal cities silhouetted ships passing along their coastlines and made the ships' movements observable to German U-boats at night.

With complete disregard for all creatures of the night, we have flooded the darkness with artificial light—great intersecting domes of light emanating from cities, suburbs, highways, and factories. Light pollution disturbs the natural rhythms of birds, insects, and nocturnal animals. For many species, light acts like a magnet. I've heard roughnecks, who work offshore on oil platforms in the Gulf of Mexico, tell stories of thousands of seabirds "captured" by the light from gas flares. The hapless birds circle and circle until they drop from exhaustion. Who hasn't seen insects cluster around streetlights? Hatchling sea turtles, naturally gravitate toward the brighter, reflective sea horizon upon hatching and are confused by artificial lighting on the shoreline. In Florida alone, hatchling losses number in the hundreds of thousands every year. Humans are diurnal creatures and have eyes adapted to living in the sun's light, but light pollution may have biological consequences for humans too. A growing body of scientific research suggests light pollution can impair biologic functions in both humans and wildlife. Researchers are working to determine the extent and nature of associations between light pollution and human health effects such as cancer, cardiovascular disease, depression, and insomnia.

Another tragic result of light pollution is that it has caused humanity to literally lose sight of its place in the universe. As a child on winter camping trips with my family, I remember feeling minuscule and insignificant when stepping away from the campfire on a crystal-clear night, looking upward to the misty river of the Milky Way, and measuring myself against the vastness of the universe. Chilled by the cold and the unfathomable sea of darkness and starlight, I would hurry back and fit myself into the ring formed by my mother and father, brother, and two sisters—all intimately gathered for the warmth and light of the fire. Staring into the pile of embers glowing like my personal mound of stars, flames flicking outward and throwing off sparks—each spark with a life of its own, each with an unpredictable destination—I would wonder at the meaning of it all.

My parents succeeded in nurturing within me a sense of wonder so deep and strong that it has practically lasted a lifetime. I remember our nighttime forays on the Gulf shore as though it were yesterday: flashlights sweeping through the darkness, searching for those aptly named elusive fleet-legged creatures rarely glimpsed in daytime—ghost crabs. It was only after Yuko's death that I began to feel world-weary and embittered. I think it was because without her companionship I no longer had someone to share the excitement and mystery of life. Tethered to a dock for an indeterminate length of time had me worrying that I would become disconnected from my remaining source of strength, the natural world. I consoled myself by savoring the cool fresh air tinged with the organic smells of low tide—that gumbo of odors of seaweeds and fishes, of exposed mud flats and decaying marsh grass, of the smells of trillions of tiny lives beginning and ending.

Maintaining a deep sense of connection was going to be a battle. I had already found myself distracted by the events of the previous day, not the least of which was feeling the allure of a beautiful woman. She was physically elegant and exuded that self-assured look of movie maidens from Hollywood's Golden Age. I hadn't felt *anything* for another woman since Yuko's death, and I was perplexed by my instant attraction to a stranger. I struggled to get her off my mind.

Finally, I was able to shift my attention to another surprising turn of events. My logical suspicion that Goose Coot was trailing Gamp had turned into confusion when, together, they greeted me the day before as I secured The Essex's mooring lines to the Last Cast's rickety pier. My suspicion was renewed when Gamp gleefully introduced him as Barzillai Ray, a bio-fuel entrepreneur out of Miami. Momentarily turning his back to Gamp, Goose gave me a knowing wink and a business card. The card read, *TermiGen: Better Living through Biochemistry.*

"TermiGen?" I asked.

"Termites. Miniature mobile bioreactors," he said, barely containing a smile. "Termites can efficiently convert lignocellulose into fermentable sugars in their digestive systems."

I decided to play along. "So, TermiGen has isolated the 500 genes in termite guts related to the enzymatic deconstruction of cellulose and hemicelluloses?"

"Ahhhh, I see you know something, Mr. Nilsson, about termite enzyme research and, of course, would more than likely know that the *real* challenge is in defining what set of genes among those 500 are the ones with key functional attributes for the breakdown of cellulose. Right?"

I expected that Goose, a nerd's nerd, would have done his homework but was curious as to how well he was prepared. "Anything related to energy alternatives to fossil fuels interests me, Mr. Ray, *and* my profession requires me to do extensive research. You're telling me that TermiGen has identified the key functional attributes for breaking down cellulose *and* determined the metabolic pathways involved in the termite's breakdown processes?"

"Wood mass to biofuel. All mapped out. Got it tested and working at industrial scale. Patent's pending. Interested in getting in on the ground floor, Mr. Nilsson?" Goose wanted to talk. "Could make you a rich man," he added.

"I'm interested, Mr. Ray," I replied, barely suppressing an urge to laugh.

"That's fantastic. You tell me when and where, and I'll be there," said Goose. "Give me a call; number's there on the card."

Gamp sensed that our exchange was concluding and spoke up. "Beers on me you two, if y'all feel like a cold one." Goose asked for a rain check and said, "I look forward to hearing from you, Mr. Nilsson," as he waddled away. I, on the other hand, was ready for something to drink and followed Gamp down the dilapidated pier and carefully picked my way up the near rotted steps to the Last Cast. As she ascended the steps, she pointed out that the second step from the top was in particularly bad shape and advised me to avoid it all together.

As we walked, I considered how best to inquire about the silver-haired beauty. When we arrived at the entrance to the Last Cast, the door flung open and a half-dozen fisherman filed out. Standing behind Gamp it was alarming to observe the volume and intensity of attention being directed at her. Each pair of male eyes flicked womanward upon clearing the doorway, the focus of each instantly changing from a semi-blank walking stare to a laser beam of heightened sexual interest. The least lascivious gave her a quick glance—the most brazen scanned her with an aggressive and openly flirtatious up-and-down appraisal. As they walked away, all swiveled their heads around at least once for a look at her ass. Admittedly, Gamp did have a nice ass. However, there was nothing about her attire or demeanor that invited the undressing she'd received. Made painfully aware by Yuko that women deal with these kinds of unsolicited visual assaults by men every minute of every day, I felt guilty because I'd behaved the same way as a younger man.

As though reading my mind, Gamp looked up at me after they'd passed and said with exasperation in her voice, "Men are all alike."

I mustered a sincere, "I know. I'm sorry."

She seemed surprised that I would cop to such a charge and lightly touching my arm responded, "I wasn't talking about you. You're not like that, Eirik."

"Maybe, but only because at my age I'm testosterone deficient," I said.

"Age has nothing to do with it," she said with a hint of affection in her eyes as we walked into the bar.

"Thanks, that's very generous of you sweetie, but if I don't have that beer soon, I'm going to sober up and fully realize that I am not only old and worn out but also flat-ass broke."

Turns out, Clara was the sole heir to a huge real estate fortune. Her grandmother and mother settled here around 1930. They owned a thousand or so acres of timberland. According to Gamp, her husband, no-good drug addict that he was, did the only generous thing he ever did for Clara and got himself killed 10 or so years ago. "Took her given name back, Butterfield, and she hasn't remarried. In fact, she doesn't seem to have much use for men. If I had her money, I don't know that I would either," Gamp said, as she leaned against the bar, her focus set somewhere out on East Bay far beyond me and the windows of the Last Cast.

Money might not be the only reason Clara didn't remarry. Only 8 percent of widows 55 to 64 remarry, and once they pass 65 only 2 percent do, I said, pulling some stats from a recent article about life after death for widows.

“Is that a fact?” Gamp, replied flatly, obviously unimpressed.

I presumed she was preoccupied with the notion of her life without a man in it. The article also offered a depressing fact about white, elderly widowers like me—they have the nation's highest suicide rates. Often, widowed men are frail and the spouse they have lost was usually their caregiver. However, it seems the most important factor in elderly widows’ faring better than elderly widowers is that these women–in contrast to men–do a better job of building a strong social network of family and friends. Numerous studies have found that two years after losing a spouse, elderly widows show no more likelihood of being depressed than other women their age. Many of them claim that after their hubbies croaked, they discovered new strengths and talents. They are even forming *tribes* around the shared sense of loss that only other widows understand—traveling together, going together to restaurants and movies, becoming caregivers for each other, sharing houses and apartments.

It *was* encouraging for me to learn that a small percentage of elderly men do fare well after the death of a spouse. These guys have developed resilience and flexibility in their lives through long experience in accepting challenges and trying out new solutions to problems. After a period of grieving the death of a beloved wife, they plunge themselves into some new and absorbing activity. I guess that would be like me if you consider my late-life love affair with dive bars to be a new and absorbing activity. I could not say, however, that I'd ever not grieve over losing Yuko. Unlike me, they quickly long for the intimacies that they believe exist for them only in a marriage or a committed relationship—usually with a considerably younger woman. I thought about this as I looked at Gamp, almost 30 years my junior, and sipped my beer.

I certainly understand being attracted to someone her age, but, aside from her relative youthfulness, she wasn't attractive to me as a potential partner. In fact, knowing that I was likely older than her father chilled me. It seems to me that the old fools who choose women for their younger faces and figures miss out on the true companionship of a contemporary—the jokes that can be understood only by those close in age; the look that passes between two people who don't have to speak a word because of age-related experiences; the literature, music, and historic events that shaped their worlds. All of which I think would be difficult, if not impossible, to enjoy with a much younger person. If some spring chicken suddenly found me brilliant, virile, witty, and charming I'd damn well know she was likely after my money—money I no longer had.

Caught up in my rumination on aging and May-and-December marriages while eyeing Gamp's body, I hadn't realized that she had turned her gaze toward me. When our eyes met, she had a what-in-the-hell-are-you-doing expression on her face. Embarrassed, I blurted, "It's not what you're thinking. If I were considering dating, hooking up, or whatever the hell they call it these days, it would be with an older woman."

"Oh, that's real flattering!" she said, with what I hoped was mock sarcasm. "That goes well on top of my butt being eyed like a pork chop. Guess I was wrong about your being different from most men. What's with you? All hopped up on your Viagra today, are ya?" I sat speechless while I felt my face grow warm and tingly. "Oh, Eirik, you're blushing! How sweet," Gamp said, in between belly laughs. "I was just fooling with you."

I didn't know whether to be angry that she was messing with my head or that she thought I was cute. "Aren't you a piece of work?" I managed, along with a grin. "A real piece of work."

"Well, it's real clear to me that you'd prefer to hook up with Clara. That's fine. My feelings are hurt, but I'll survive," she teased. "In fact, she wants to meet you too. She asked if I would explore the possibility of your talking to her reading club, The Wetumpka Book Club, about your latest novel at their next meeting."

It was true that I was interested in meeting Clara, but I wasn't prepared to have the prospect of that happening to be thrust upon me so suddenly. I'd fantasized that I would attend some event where I'd be able to observe her in a social setting before attempting conversation.

"Of course. Yes, of course," I stuttered. "Let her know that I'd be delighted. Will you arrange it?"

"Yep, I'll take care of it, I'll set it all up," Gamp said. I had a sneaking suspicion that it was *all* a set up.

"Wetumpka?"

"Creek Indian word for rumbling water," was her answer.

Before getting back to The Essex, I finished one beer and had another plus a shot of tequila. I don't think that I have a particularly acute sense of smell *except* when it comes to cigarette smoke. For some reason I'm a scent hound when someone lights up, and someone in the near vicinity of The Essex had done just that. The acrid bite of burning tobacco snaking up my nose abruptly commanded my attention. Curious, I studied the water around the stern area of The Essex. Not seeing anything, I quietly headed up the starboard side towards the bow. Nothing. As I headed down the port side, I noticed a dingy tied up to a piling underpinning the Last Cast. I hadn't heard anyone paddle up, but given my diminished hearing, that didn't surprise me. No one was in the dingy. I guessed that they'd lit up after stepping ashore. *Probably came in off a sailboat anchored out of sight of The Essex*, I thought. As I headed back to my deck chair, the smell of cigarette grew stronger. Smoke was wafting around the corner of the aft cabin. Only one person I know would have the audacity to do such a thing. Either it was Goose, or, if not, I was about to get my ass wacked.

"Evening Air Wick, saw your cabin lights." Air Wick was the nickname Goose stuck on me years ago. It started as a dig on my aftershave. "Was having a hard time sleeping myself. Thought you'd like a little company," Goose said as he pinched off the glowing tip of his cigarette between the thumb and forefinger of his right hand, flicked it into the river, and pocketed the stub.

Although not best friends, we shared a common bond that transcended our differences. I trusted him, and it felt good to see a familiar face. He was also an odd bird, smart as hell, and fun to be around. We shook hands. "What in the Sam Hill are you up to now Goose," I asked as I pulled over a deck chair and gestured for him to have a seat. But, before you answer that, can I interest you in a couple of shots of Sammy Hagger's finest anejo?

"Absolutely," he answered with a smile.

"You got a grin on you like a possum eating persimmons, Goose. I don't think I've ever seen you feeling quite so fine," I said. Goose, born and raised in Alabama, was an aficionado of southern expressions and whenever we got together, they'd start popping out of us. "Finer than frog hair, Eirik. Yes, sir. Feeling *finer* than frog hair."

CHAPTER 6

"Frannnnkly. . .my dearrrr. . I. . .I. . .d. .. d. .don't. . .WANT A DAM," Goose said, in what I guessed was an impersonation of Clara Butterfield making it known that she was lending her substantial financial support to FLOW. We had been talking and drinking tequila all night, and he was slurring and stumbling. I'd seen Goose annihilated by alcohol before. A benign drunk, unlike me, he rarely makes an ass out of himself. Typically, he falls asleep, and this time was no different. His eye lids fluttered a few times before shutting, followed by a long exhalation while his chin slowly descended to his chest. It was like watching an infant fall asleep—a few involuntary twitches of limb and lip and he was out. Careful not to startle him, I grasped his shot glass and gently tugged it out of his hand.

Dammed up by a low cloud hugging the eastern shore of the bay, the early morning sunlight suddenly brimmed over the cloud top and spilled across the aft deck of The Essex—dazzling brilliance. Sudden shadows of pelicans in flight glided across Goose's lap. As I looked up and out across the bay toward the sun, I had the disconcerting sensation that the earth was rolling—rolling with me towards the horizon and into the fiery morning light. *Heart attack?* I panicked in silence. Most likely lack of sleep and too much tequila, I concluded after steadying myself. I needed some food and a couple of cups of coffee. I nudged Goose to see if he had any interest in breakfast. He was dead to the world. I stuck a note on my chair letting him know I would be at the Bakin' and Eggs, should he wake and want to join me.

The Bakin' was packed and buzzing. While waiting to order, I overheard that there'd been some sort of accident on the coast road the day before. Quizzing my waitress, I learned that two men had been killed by a falling tree east of town on Highway 98. A powerful gust of wind had snapped off the top of large pine tree which then fell on top of the car of the two unsuspecting victims as they drove by. "Killed instantly," she said, shaking her head. "When your time's up. . ."

Killed instantly! That is what I was told about Yoku's death. At the time I believed it. But, weeks later when I could think again, I began to consider the circumstances of her death. I realized that "killed instantly" was just another one of those supposed palliative phrases in the same family as: "Time will heal, there's no sense dwelling on the past" and the two that would instantly enrage me, "I know how you feel" and "God never gives us more than we can handle." "Killed instantly," said the friend who delivered the news of Yoku's death, attempting to assure me that she didn't suffer. I would have preferred to believe that she didn't suffer, but no one really knew what she was feeling in her last moments. I know now that my friend's intentions were good and he, along with many others, was simply inept when it came to dealing with my grief. Worse than all the clichés, was the conspiracy of silence when I eventually did return to the office. With one exception, Dario, the guy who emptied the wastebaskets at the end of each day, everyone else avoided mentioning Yoku's death. Dario said, "I am so sorry, Mr. Nilsson. I don't know what to say. I feel so bad for you." His simple offering of sorry breached my despair and for a moment I didn't feel so alone. I offered to buy him a drink, but he was just starting his second job of the day and wouldn't be off until midnight.

Goose understood. A few years before Yoku was killed, his wife of 16 years went into cardiac arrest and died while he slept next to her. She had been only 40 and remarkably fit with no history of heart problems. When I told him about Yoku' s death, the first thing he said was, "You're going to think this is bullshit, but you're going to be fine, Eirik. Something bad can lead to something good. You gotta be open to accepting it." I knew he was speaking from personal experience, so I listened as he told his story. He never said that his partner had died nor that she had passed away, another euphemism I disliked. Instead, Goose said, "When my wife disappeared..." That was exactly how it felt to me too. Yoku disappeared and with her so did our plans and dreams, our morning pillow talk, our goodnight kisses. Everything we enjoyed doing together. Everything good. All gone—just like *that.*

With a cup of tea and a copy of the *New York Times* in hand, after breakfast I moved outdoors into the Bakin's courtyard to a bistro table shaded by an ancient Dogwood tree. I needed to get started on my next novel and, believing that truth is stranger than fiction, was using the paper primarily to stimulate my imagination. It's a serendipitous method I've employed for years. I let the creative, right side of my brain roam while the rational, left side stands back observing what captures the right side's attention — "*Ethics for Extraterrestrials,*" "*Southeast Drought Study Ties Water Shortage to Population, Not Global Warming,*" "*More With Dementia Wander from Home,*" "*River Basin Fight Pits Atlanta Against Neighbors,*" "*Moonshine Finds New Craftsmen and Enthusiasts,*" "*No Fooling with Mother Nature,*" "*Chimps Use Tools to Help with their Sex Lives.*" Chimps would probably have been the more entertaining topic but probably the least productive, so I started with *River Basin Fight.* I had no doubt it was about the Apalachicola, Chattahoochee, and Flint River Basin water war, which I was beginning to think might be a fertile context for my story. Like most water wars, this one pitted developer against environmentalist and state against state—in this case, Florida, Georgia, and Alabama. The big difference was that it was taking place in the normally verdant southeast, not the water-parched southwest. Due to a drought of historic proportions, water supplies were rapidly shrinking, and North Georgia was under severe water restrictions. Officials were warning that Lake Lanier, a 38,000-acre reservoir that supplies more than 3 million Atlanta residents with water, was less than three months from depletion.

What originally fired-up my imagination was a scene broadcast on every major network that I could not have written better. Backed up by a choir singing "Amazing Grace," Georgia's Baptist Governor, Sonny Perdue, accompanied by three Protestant ministers, led hundreds in a prayer for rain. "We've come together here," he said, "simply for one reason and one reason only: to very reverently and respectfully pray up a storm." Standing nearby were 20 protestors from the Atlanta Freethought Society who opposed the rain prayer. Their spokesperson stated to the reporter, "The governor can pray when he wants to. What he can't do is lead prayers in the name of the people of Georgia." The governor, an Elmer Fudd look-alike wearing a University-of-Georgia-red suit and black cowboy boots, obviously believed that not only could he petition God in the name of Georgia with impunity, he could also shamelessly insult Georgia Tech fans.

The governor's plea to God to bless Atlanta with a thunderstorm or two went unanswered, and he resorted to asking a federal judge to force the Army Corps of Engineers to curb the amount of water it releases from Lake Lanier into rivers flowing down to Florida. The Chattahoochee and Flint Rivers converge at the Georgia-Florida border to form the Apalachicola River. Florida countered by suing the Corps claiming that it was violating the federal Endangered Species Act with its plans to limit flows of water from northern Georgia into the Apalachicola-Chattahoochee-Flint River Basin. “The Corps’ operations continue to jeopardize the threatened Gulf sturgeon, endangered fat three ridge mussel, and threatened purple bank climber mussel,” the suit claimed. It was ruled that the Corps had been illegally reallocating water to meet metro Atlanta’s needs.

Georgia promptly appealed the ruling, and a prominent U.S. Senator from Georgia retaliated against Florida with threats to boycott the annual Georgia-Florida football game played in Jacksonville. "There is no logical reason why we should encourage Georgians every year to spend millions of dollars in Florida, work to fill their tax coffers, and then find their revenue being used to destroy the economy of North Georgia in a federal district court,” he said. The game sold out and Florida beat the crap out of Georgia. Clearly, God was standing with the state of Florida, the University of Florida, the Apalachicola River, the fat three ridge, *and* the purple bank climber. Desperate for water, Georgia resuscitated a 100-year-old dispute with Tennessee over an 1818 land survey maintaining that the survey was inaccurate and marked the border south of where it should be. In the Georgia Senate, lawmakers broke into a rendition of "This Land is My Land," as Sen. David Shafer stood up to speak. Shafer introduced a resolution that would establish Georgia's northern boundary about a mile farther north into what is now Tennessee — giving Georgia access to the massive Tennessee River.

As far as subject matter goes, it did not get much juicier. Regardless, I was still facing at least 18 months of painstaking grit and grind at the keyboard. Novel number 12, published before I lost Yuko and my fortune, was no easier than my first. There was every reason for me to believe that 13 was going to be an especially hard row. Nearly broke and with book sales flagging, I really didn't have a choice. I called Charles, my agent, and let him know I was pulling up anchor and hoisting the main, our timeworn signal that I was ready to start working. He was delighted by the news and responded as he always did by wishing me, "fair winds and following seas and long may your big jib draw."

Ending my call to Charles, I returned to the *Times*. Midway through the arts section, I began to experience that vague feeling of uneasiness I get when someone is staring at me. Being gawked at was something that happened on occasion when I was in New York making the talk show rounds and pitching my latest work. Peeking over the top of my paper, I met Clara Butterfield's eyes. My heart literally skipped a beat. I don't know how long she'd been sitting at the table opposite of mine. She was looking at me with a determined look. Her platinum gray hair was pulled backed tightly into a ponytail and she was dressed comfortably and simply—light-weight black sweater, khaki-colored pants, and what looked like canvas-topped riding boots. Could have been L.L. Bean or Prada as far as I knew—I'm no fashionista—but whatever the brand, it all fit her perfectly.

"Why, Mr. Nilsson, what a coincidence that I would run into you. I'm Clara—Clara Butterfield. I was just speaking to my dear friend, Gamp, and was happy to learn that you have agreed to speak to our book club," she said, her azure blue eyes fixed on me. Azure is often described as the color of the sky on a clear day.

Her speech had a low-pitched quality that reminded me of Lauren Bacall's husky, seductive voice. The effect of years of smoking, I suspected. Her lightly tanned skin was silky smooth however, and obviously not that of a smoker. It seemed to me she had no makeup on. But Yuko, who stopped wearing makeup when she turned forty, once pointed out to me that a great makeup job was one that highlighted the strongest features of the wearer, and concealed the weakest, without drawing attention to the makeup itself. Whatever the case, I was taken by Clara's beauty. I had no idea how much time had passed before I realized with a start that I had not spoken.

Somewhere deep inside my psyche my mother took control and ordered me to behave like the gentlemen she raised me to be. I obediently stood up, tucked my *Times* under my left arm for God knows what reason, walked over to Clara Butterfield's table, and stiffly extended my right hand while exclaiming, "It's a pleasure to meet you Ms. Butterfield, please join me . . . at *my* table."

She seemed amused and studied me for a moment more as I stood there, my hand hanging limply out in space. To my great relief, she finally took my hand into both of hers and said, "It's a pleasure to meet you too, *Mr. Nilsson*, but please, why don't you join me...at *my* table? After all, you've already here, newspaper and all." As I began to seat myself, I felt my cheeks burning. "Mr. Nilsson, you're... how sweet! I can't remember the last time I saw a grown man *blush*," she cooed."

"Eirik, please call me Eirik, Ms. Butterfield," I replied, struggling to regain some degree of composure as I squirmed in my chair.

"Of course, and I'd be delighted if you call me Clara. Oh, here comes my breakfast. Would you care for something else to eat or drink, Eirik?" I didn't realize she'd not been served and, feeling I was intruding, began to stand up and excuse myself. "Sit down, Eirik, and please stop trying so hard to be the perfect gentlemen. We have so much to talk about," she said firmly but with a broad smile, "like Barzillai Ray the termite-man. Such an unusual name, Barzillai, isn't it? Had to Google that one and guess what I discovered?" She raised her eyebrows and looked at me expectantly.

"You really want me to guess," I replied.

“Well, honestly, I’m feeling pretty confident that you don’t have to guess; that you know the answer,” she said as she spread a thin layer of jam across a piece of toast. “Being the literary lion you are, I think you gave some thought to naming that exquisite houseboat of yours—The Essex. Why you would choose the name of the only whaling ship known to be sunk by a sperm whale, I have no idea. I’m sure you have your reasons though. But that sad story did inspire Herman Melville to write Moby Dick, didn’t it?”

“What are you getting at, Ms. Butterfield,” I said even though I knew what she was suggesting.

“You don’t mean to tell me that you don’t know that Barzillai Ray was one of the sailors on The Essex who, after the whale sunk it, was later eaten by his stranded and starving shipmates,” she said with a bit of exasperation in her voice.

“Of course, I know that, but what does that have to do with anything,” I said, starting to feel uncomfortable.

“It has to do with my thinking that you know that Barzillai Ray is not that termite gentlemen’s real name. It has to do with *my* knowing that the two of you spent the better part of the night together like long lost friends catching up on old times. It has to do with that man acting way too eager to get to know me and all my friends. I’ve got the means to find out who he really is and what he’s up to, Eirik, but I figure you can save me a whole lot of time and money by just telling me.” She took a bite of toast, which she held in her left hand, and slowly chewed. In her right hand she lightly tapped out with her knife an impatient little rhythm on the edge of her plate. She was waiting for a response.

I'd learned from Goose that he was still with the ATF and had been placed in Apalachicola to investigate the Tupelo Alliance, a tax-exempt, environmental organization suspected of funneling money to support FLOW's southeastern "frontline" activists—the "monkeywrenchers" who blow things up. However, the company he was representing, TermiGen, was a legitimate business and not just a front for his ATF activities and I didn't need to lie about that. Gamp obviously could see whatever I was doing from her roost at the Last Cast and had reported my activities to Clara. Knowing this fed into my paranoia about living in small towns, and I couldn't help but think I was being manipulated; for what reason, I didn't have a clue. Regardless, unless she was eavesdropping too, Gamp would not know what Goose and I were talking about.

Risking that she wasn't listening in, I replied, "It's been my experience, Clara, that sharing a bottle of tequila can quickly take the business out of any business meeting. As far as The Essex is concerned, she was named after my favorite hotel in Chicago. Has nothing to do with the whaling ship, Barzillai Ray, or Herman Melville," I lied. "I must confess though, when I am working on a novel, everyone I meet has the potential to become a character in my story," I said, hoping to distract her. Mr. Ray is a character in his own right. How he came about having the same name of a man eaten by his shipmates, I have no idea. That said, I feel certain I will want to spend more time with him. Call it research. Who knows, maybe he'll even tell me the story behind his name."

Having finished her toast, Clara cradled her coffee cup in both hands as she sipped and considered my response before speaking. "Forgive me, Eirik, for being so pushy. Your affairs are really none of my business. Sadly, it seems that as my wealth has grown, I've become more and more suspicious of peoples' motives. Enough of me and my paranoia, though; I want to know more about your next novel. *But* first, let's set a date for you to meet with my little book club."

I guessed she was lying about her reasons for being suspicious, but she seemed genuinely contrite. *Filthy rich, clever, and beautiful—many a seasoned sailor had been drawn upon rocky shoals by the allure of a lesser siren,* I thought. The Want in my heart at that moment had grown large. Reason was warning me not to do anything foolish. Years of damned up feelings were yearning to burst through my grief and guilt, and I knew that when it came to Clara Butterfield, I was not going to listen to Reason. I had lived in the past long enough.

CHAPTER 7

According to Goose, it was a developer's proposal to site a 200-unit apartment complex on land surrounded by Ogeechee tupelos that pushed Wewahitchka's beekeepers into forming the Tupelo Alliance. The expansive floodplain forest of the Apalachicola River ranks among the richest natural habitats on Earth. Ogeechee tupelo, *nyssa aquatica,* one of more than forty kinds of trees in the floodplain, grows particularly well in the moist, acidic soil around the small river town of Wewahitchka. Wewahitcha is said to be an Indian term meaning "water eyes." Locals have whittled it down to "Wewa." Wewa is set back from the west bank of the Apalachicola River about fifty miles upriver from the town of Apalachicola. Beekeeping has been a way of life there for generations. Honeybees feast on tupelo blossoms during the short blooming season from late April to May. When the massive bloom ends, and the tupelo flowers begin to drop, beekeepers race to strip the honey from the hives before the bees can taint the pure tupelo with nectar from swamp titi, high-bush gall berry, Yaupon holly, or wild rosemary blossoms. Because the beehives are placed on elevated platforms along difficult-to-reach edges of the river, gathering tupelo honey is a sometimes dangerous, always laborious, and therefore expensive, process. Regardless, season after season demand outstrips the supply and honey-lovers around the world pay top dollar for it. However, tupelo honey production, which contributes over 2 million dollars annually to the local economy, was being threatened.

The Alliance's first action was to pool their resources and hire an environmental legal eagle out of Tallahassee to block the development. The developer prevailed but only after a bitter and protracted battle between the "pro-bees-ness" locals who wanted to preserve Wewa's rural ways and the pro-business "trespassers" who envisioned Wewa as the ideal setting for an upscale hunting and fishing retreat. As the project neared completion, late one night, a spectacular fire reduced all 200 units to piles of smoldering ash. It was reported that flames leapt hundreds of feet into the air and could be seen for miles. A cyclonic vortex of embers swirled upward in the night with such force that it stripped pinecones from nearby pine trees, set them ablaze, and dropped them like miniature firebombs upon the little town. Residents on the perimeter of the site, who had been evacuated, returned home to find the siding on their houses, although hundreds of feet away from the inferno, charred or melted from the intense heat. Everyone who could read knew it was arson. A crudely lettered sign planted at the project's entrance stated defiantly: "The bees are mad as hell and they're not going to take it anymore." Lost on many of the locales was the "bees" implied reference to the satirical film "Network." A big fan of Paddy Chayefsky, the film's screenwriter, Goose enjoyed the dark humor of the sign's author.

In the investigation that followed, everyone affiliated with the Tupelo Alliance, which was virtually every family in Wewa, was detained and interrogated—everyone that could be found. Law enforcement authorities searched high and low for Owen Coughlin. Owen was better known in Wewa as Father Fury, a nickname he picked up when he served as Catholic chaplain in the Iraq war. Before being ordained a priest and volunteering to serve in the military, he had served as a corrections officer at the county jail. Goose described him as a sturdy man, compact and burly in the bulky way of a schoolyard bully, with thick, shoulder-length black hair and a bent nose that could pass for a Bronx street fighter's. Many of the people Goose interviewed during his investigation said they were shocked when Owen entered the seminary. Seems he had been raised Baptist and after graduating high school was rarely seen in church. However, none were surprised that, when his unit was engaged in a fierce firefight, he had picked up the rifle of a mortally wounded soldier he was administering the last rites to and put to eternal rest a half-dozen enemy soldiers.

Shortly thereafter, Owen left the priesthood and the Church. Returning to Wewa, he quietly built a rough, single-room cabin high up on stilts at a site deep in the floodplain where he took up beekeeping. When investigators went out to question Owen, they had a difficult time locating his cabin. No one was willing to assist them, and Goose finally had to call in an ATF helicopter to search the area with thermal sensors. They eventually found the cabin and his hives but not Owen. Goose believed that Owen was the arsonist, but other than his suspicious disappearance, no concrete evidence was found that would officially implicate him. Even though he would never admit it, my gut told me that Goose was secretly rooting for Owen—his David in a backwoods David and Goliath story. He'd heard rumors that Owen had been sighted working a pair of oyster tongs out on Apalachicola Bay and felt that he was still close by hiding out in the floodplain, living off the land and the generosity of those in Wewa who held him up as their hero.

Goose was deeply upset about the possibility of the Tupelo Alliance being mixed up with FLOW's eco-saboteurs. If it were true that the Alliance was laundering money for the purpose of eco-sabotage, all associated could be charged with racketeering or even worse, supporting terrorism. Given that practically everyone in the little village was involved with the Alliance in one way or another, such a charge would devastate many families and leave Wewa looking like a ghost town. What didn't make sense to me was what they might be targeting. After all, they had already chased off the real estate developers. Goose wasn't absolutely certain, but the intelligence he was getting was suggesting that FLOW wanted to blow up one or more dams in the Apalachicola-Chattahoochee-Flint (ACF) river basin. I said that given FLOW was openly advocating de-licensing and decommissioning Jim Woodruff dam at the head of the Apalachicola River, wouldn't it be disingenuous on their part to try to destroy it or any dam in the basin? Goose responded that it wasn't uncommon for radical environmental groups to combine more traditional legal tactics with "direct action" and that they were extremely diligent when it came to covering their tracks. "It's very rare that the street activists are involved in covert, direct acts," he explained.

What I still didn't understand was what Wewa's beekeepers had against dams. Goose schooled me, "You don't get enough water flowing down the river and plant and animal species that require seasonal flooding begin to die back or they get encroached upon by other species that the flooding normally drowns out." Apparently, Ogeechee tupelo is one of those species. He went on, "Even with 13 dams and the like on the ACF, everything worked well until the 80s when Atlanta boomed and demand for water skyrocketed. Large farming concerns below Atlanta were also beginning to make a big hit on the water coming down the Basin. That demand combined with a few severe droughts in a row and the Corp of Engineers—who controls who gets how much water— playing favorites, and you got yourself a water war. Take the dams out of the equation, and the river goes back to flowing like it has for thousands of years and all the fishes and oysters and trees downstream, and the people who depend on them for a living, are happy. Upstream though, you got millions of city folks screaming bloody murder and the State of Georgia threatening to call out their National Guard."

I guess I was silent for too long as I thought about what the beekeepers were up against, as well as what FLOW and Clara might be up to, and my silence was making Goose fidgety. He lightly tapped his drink glass on the arm of his deck chair as he scanned the horizon on the east side of the bay. Standing up, he walked to the stern of The Essex and looked upriver and then down river. Turning suddenly, he looked over at me and said in an exaggerated Southern drawl, "So, whacha thinkin', cuzzzz?" I knew I couldn't match the carefully crafted accent, but I gave it my best and said that I didn't know whether to scratch my watch or wind my butt. I guess it wasn't good enough. Goose blinked hard a couple of times, looked away with mock disgust and said, "Just 'cause you was born in the South don't make you Southern, ya know? My dawg sleeps in the garage. Don't make him a truck."

"Seriously Eirik, I'm curious to know what you're thinking," he said while holding his glass out at eye level and gently swirling the tequila around. "I'm guessing you're thinking about that Butterfield woman. You didn't see me at the Bakin' but I saw you two. I saw how you were looking at her and the way she was looking at you. Listen to me! What you do with her is none of my business, but as a friend I'm warning you to be careful, be very careful."

“What do you know, Goose,” I asked?

“I’m not, I can’t. . . I’m just doing my job. You of all people should know and respect that.”

“Of course, I do Goose,” I said. I felt badly that if I befriended Clara, it would put him in a difficult position. I would have to heed his warning though; although a compassionate man, he was also highly ethical, and I had no doubt that if I got sideways with the law he would arrest me. He wouldn’t feel good about it, but he would do it.

Later that evening as he was leaving, he stepped onto the dock and stood there awhile, dredged his car keys out his pocket and nervously jangled them before saying, “Eirik?”

I replied, “Yes, Goose.”

He continued, “I’m not going to look the other way, you know?”

I said, “I know, you’ve got a job to do.”

He nodded, starting walking away and then stopped and turned. “Promise me one thing,” he said.

“What’s that?”

“Promise me if you find out she’s up to no good that you’ll have the good sense to save your own ass. I don’t expect you to turn her in or anything, just get the fuck out of the way and save your ass, okay?"

"I think we're both getting way ahead of ourselves, Goose," I said. "Don't worry, I'll be fine. All she wants from me is to talk to her book club." He grinned, shook his head slowly from side to side, and resumed walking.

As a boy I used to wonder how it was that every one of the endless flows of old men seeking retirement paradise in South Florida didn't care about the thick tufts of course hair sprouting from their ears and nostrils or the oily scales of detritus littering their eyeglasses. I construed their lack of vanity as a sign they'd given up on themselves and thought them gross and pitiable. I've come to realize from my own experience that old age is a goddam shipwreck, and in most cases, it probably wasn't for a lack of caring for themselves, but a by-product of diminished eyesight. I rarely look at myself in the mirror anymore except to shave, but when I do, I use a 15-power magnifying mirror. The first time I used it I nearly had a stroke. Where a reflection of my face should have been was a relief map—a rough-hewn landscape of sunbaked skin, cracked and creased, and run through with canyon-like ruts, all of which was traversed by a complex road system of fine red lines drawn with the ink of broken capillaries; worse than that was discovering a miniature forest of boar-like bristles growing out of each of my ears. Age had taken me by surprise. I had become an unrecognizable, alien version of myself and yet within myself I felt I had not changed—much.

Sometimes when Yoku thought I was being too critical of my aging body she talked about a concept so deeply embedded in Japanese culture that she had a difficult time explaining it in Western terms. She called it Wabi-sabi and defined it for me in writing so I might actually "get it."

She wrote, "Wabi and Sabi were originally two separate Japanese aesthetic concepts. Over time, the two were combined to form one word. Basically, Wabi is about simplicity and quietude, and incorporates the idea of rustic beauty. It can apply to natural things as well as manmade. Sabi is about things both natural and manmade whose beauty stems from natural aging and the concept that changes brought upon by use make an object more beautiful and valuable. Sabi also incorporates an appreciation of the cycles of life and reminds us that we are all transient beings on this planet—that our bodies, as well as the material world around us, are in the process of returning to dust."

I eventually came to understand Wabi-sabi as a world view centered on the acceptance of transience and imperfection. Knowing that I understood Nature's cycles of growth, decay, and death, Yoku encouraged me to see and accept those same cycles in my own body. However, my upbringing ran contrary to accepting myself as I am—that no matter how many self-improvements I could rack up, I was taught that there is always room for more improvement. The practice of Wabi-sabi also seemed to require developing an ability to slow down, to shift from doing to being, to appreciating rather than perfecting. Although appealing, it sounded like what I might aspire to in retirement. When working at the *Journal*, I'd practically be out of my mind with boredom after a two-week vacation break.

Wabi-sabi came effortlessly and naturally to Yoku, and I'm certain that it had much to do with what I loved about her. When I talked to Goose about it, his opinion was that I was too set in my Western ways to change and joked that I really was more of a Wabi-*sama* than a Wabi-*sabi* kind of guy. Sama is a Japanese honorific sometimes added after a person's name for whom there is great respect or admiration. Mimicking the formality of a Japanese tea ceremony when preparing to share a bottle of Cabo Wabo tequila, Goose once bowed deeply before me saying in all seriousness, "Konnichi wa, Eirik-sama." Being a two-man admiration society, I bowed in kind and replied, Konnichi wa, Goosi-sama.

When living upriver on The Essex I generally shaved before going into Apalachicola for supplies—about once a week. Looking "presentable" in public had been hammered deep into my psyche by my father. I also didn't like the feel of a beard and wouldn't allow more than a week's growth to accumulate on my face. It was time for a shave, I thought to myself as I lathered my face; it was simply coincidence that speaking to the Wetumpka book club fell on shaving day. But honestly, I knew I wanted to look my best for Clara.

Deciding what to wear was another issue. I didn't want to appear too casual, yet I also didn't want to overdress. Yuko liked seeing me in snug-fitting jeans; a crisp, white, pima cotton sport shirt with an open collar; a pair of obscenely expensive calfskin, Italian loafers that I bought on impulse one summer in Rome; and a perfectly tailored English tweed shooting jacket that she gave me on my 55th birthday. She said the style that suited me best was "sporty"—casual, comfortable clothes in natural fabrics. Knowing how quickly fashions can change, I hoped that what was sporty a few years ago was not now farty-old-man. Regardless, I couldn't pick out for myself what to wear with any measure of confidence, so I went with what Yuko thought looked good on me.

I may have had zero style-sense when I was younger, but I rarely felt unattractive. The thought that at I was too old to hope I could be found desirable crossed my mind. I felt unsettled as I walked out onto Water Street and stood in front of The Last Cast where Clara was having me picked up. I'd seen it happen all too often with my male friends and knew without a doubt that there is no age limit for men to make fools of themselves. I also knew there is nothing in the world more pathetic than a delusional old fool who is not aware that he is delusional, old, or a fool.

I felt certain Clara *and* Gamp had something in mind for me, and my curiosity was piqued. Plus, I was surprised and fascinated by my spontaneous attraction to another woman for the first time since losing Yuko. I couldn't imagine ever letting go of my love for Yuko or loving anyone the way I loved her. Shortly after Yuko died, Goose had advised me to give myself plenty of time to grieve and not to jump into a new relationship—not that I wanted to. He said when I did eventually find myself attracted to someone new, I shouldn't compare the depth of feelings I had for Yuko with her. I knew that was advice I could trust. He had certainly been right when he said that I would adapt and learn to live with my grief and that with each passing year those debilitating bouts of sadness would occur less frequently. That fact aside, I didn't know if I was ready to try balancing what Yuko and I had with giving my heart to a new relationship. I decided that the only way to find out was to put it out there and try. Nothing ventured, nothing gained, I assured myself as a young man driving a gleaming, white SUV pulled to the curb precisely at 3:00 P.M. As I approached the vehicle, he stepped out, opened the rear door, and politely invited me to make myself comfortable.

CHAPTER 8

"That money pit; I'm thinking about shipping it back to Japan! Freestone was obsessed with Aikido and Japanese culture, and before you could say yakitori, a bunch of eight-wheelers pull up one afternoon packing a 300-year-old, farmhouse. You know anything about Japanese architecture? Gassho zukuri-style?" Yoku's family home was built in the Gassho zukuir style. I nodded yes. "As cold-hearted as this may sound Eirik, the day he died was the most liberating of my life! The worthless, son-of-a-bitch tormented me and everyone else who had the great misfortune to be charmed into his harebrained schemes! That he wasn't murdered was the only surprise greater than his losing a race with a freight train. *That* wasn't much of a surprise because everyone predicted that he'd die doing something idiotic during one of his frequent binges." I sat in stunned silence as Clara broke her tirade just long enough to take a big swig of gin and tonic.

"I knew he was seriously addicted to something, but even I was shocked after the police cut through the twisted metal that had been a gorgeous Porsche Cayenne. They discovered more hits of mescaline than you could count, a huge ice chest full of cocaine, another big chest stuffed with grass, hundreds of uppers and downers, $100,000 in hundred-dollar bills, *and* a case of Don Julio Gonzalez tequila that, unlike Freestone, miraculously escaped the impact. Inky Parramore, the police officer who delivered the news, said that he died instantly."

I eyed the crystal snifter from which I was sipping some exceptionally smooth tequila and wondered if it was from the miracle case. "That snifter you're holding there--$350 a pair. Freestone had to have them. Bought a dozen. Just two left. Smashed all the others in the fireplace," Clara said. "Hand blown, and hand cut by Czech glass masters using only the finest European crystal. Had to be the finest. Always the *finest*. That was Freestone. Wouldn't be right to drink $300-dollar-a-bottle tequila out of anything else he would say." All I could offer in response was a feeble, "I'm sorry." "So am I, Eirik. Don't get me wrong, though; I'm not bitter about the money. God knows he went through it like a shark through a chum slick, but I still have more than I can spend in the time I have left on this Earth. It's the 10 years of my life that I wasted thinking I could fix him—that's what makes me so damn mad."

Gamp had made it clear that Clara didn't grieve Freestone's death. What I didn't expect was that simply expressing my surprise at seeing an authentic, traditional rural Japanese home in North Florida, thatched roof and all, would trigger such an angry rant. It was beautifully sited down by the river, and I had hoped that if I asked about it, Clara would offer to show me the interior. After sitting in silence for a while she calmly said, "Sorry to dump all that emotional crap on you, Eirik. Obviously, you touched a raw nerve. I've got someone, a friend, living down there right now. He's a very private man; otherwise, I'd say look around. Hell, if he weren't there already, you'd be welcome to live there." I wondered what her relationship with this guy was. Surely, he was not a renter; she obviously didn't need money.

I hadn't noticed the house before in my comings and goings in The Essex and guessed it was because of the cluster of mature Weeping Willows it was nestled in. I decided I'd pay closer attention on my next trip upriver. With their limbs gracefully arching down and sweeping the ground, willows have always reminded me of ballet dancers. My first impression of Clara from a distance was similar. Judging from her appearance, I assumed she would be all grace and refinement like a ballerina. I would have never guessed she had such a crusty, old-salt type of personality.

I was intrigued by the contrast in her appearance and behavior and wanted more than ever to get to know her better. Unsure of myself about where to even begin a conversation, I'd done a little online research into what questions to ask when wanting to get to know someone new. In one relationship and dating forum someone suggested: "Where do you live? What do you do for fun or profit? Have you always lived here? Do you have relatives here? Do you have friends here that I might know? Do you believe in magic? How did you get so beautiful, tall, good looking?" I'd thought them to be rather innocuous icebreakers, but they all seemed terribly insipid in that moment as I scrambled for a response to Clara's apology and a way to change the subject.

I was appalled to hear myself say, "Please, Clara, no need to apologize. . .Uh, what do you do for fun? She quietly studied me for a moment through the bottoms of her bifocals, her chin tucked downward toward her chest. Then, she slowly raised her head upward as she simultaneously lifted her right hand to her face, propped her elbow on the arm of her chair, laid her pointer finger alongside the right side of her jaw, and finally rested her chin on her thumb. The longer she held that pose, the more I feared my social ineptitude had whiplashed her fine mind into catatonia.

"My god, Eirik, no one has asked me that question in decades! How lovely! I'll tell you what I like doing more than anything else: I absolutely love to fly. In fact, let's go flying now. The weather is glorious!"

"What about your book club," I asked?

"Forgive me Eirik, I should have said something when you first arrived, but it seems as though most of the gals in my group have succumbed to a bug that's making the rounds," she said. "Would you mind terribly if we postponed your talk to a time when everyone is feeling better? I'll let them know we're not meeting and then we'll fly over to one of my favorite restaurants. That would be so much more *fun* than having dinner here at home. Are you game?"

At that point it was I who was experiencing whiplash. One moment I'm expecting to address a women's book club and the next Clara is inviting me to fly off to who-knows-where for dinner. The ten questions that simultaneously sprung up in my head were each clamoring for an answer, and I was having difficulty putting them into any logical order. What came out first was, "Fly?"

"Yes, fly. I pilot my own Beechcraft Baron G58. She'll get us to New Orleans in less than two hours. Are you comfortable with that, Eirik," she asked? "Did you think I meant commercial, she quickly added." I did think that, or she had her own pilot. It didn't occur to me that she meant she would literally fly the plane. I'd been a passenger in all manner of general aviation planes, from single engine to corporate jets, and wouldn't have been uncomfortable flying in her plane, which I knew to be the standard bearer among twin-engine aircraft. Being highly aware of how age had diminished my own sight and reaction speed, I was stuck on Clara's age, and hesitated a moment before answering.

It was time enough for her to read my mind. "Shame on you! You're wondering if I'm too old to be a pilot, aren't you?"

“That’s not what I was thinking at all, I said. You were right the first time; I *was* wondering if you meant commercial.”

She stood up, walked over to where I was sitting, put her hand on my arm, gently squeezed it, smiled warmly, and said, “It’s so surprising to me that a hugely successful fiction writer can be such an inept liar. From here on out it will serve you well to remember that for over a decade I lived with someone who had great difficulty telling the truth. I learned how to read a lie, no matter how big or small, coming from a mile away. Jesus, you’re blushing again. That’s another dead giveaway. Stop worrying, you’re in luck. The G58 has a state-of-the-art emergency auto landing system on board—one of just a few in the country in a plane like mine. In fact, this thing can be programed to take off on auto too. Practically a drone. I’ll just need to show you how to activate the system.

I thought this could be one of those pivotal moments in a new relationship that sets its course, so I came clean. I confessed that it was true that I was thinking her age might compromise her ability to fly an airplane safely but only because of my own creeping decrepitude. She replied with a hint of indignation in her voice, “Piloting a plane is as natural to me as driving, and I’m still a *damn* good driver. I’m not about ready to give up the keys to my car, are *you*? Thoroughly embarrassed and humiliated for being called on a form of discrimination that I had frequently taken other people to task on, I apologized.

She was quick to forgive me—quicker than I was to forgive her an hour later when, cruising at 18,000 feet, she convincingly faked a heart attack and freaked me out. But the wicked old prankster's laughter was so infectious I couldn't remain angry, and I laughed along with her. It was in that bright, mirthful moment, alone with her high above the Earth when I realized it would be easy for me to fall in love. Instantly, I was filled with dread—I didn't want to suffer losing a loved one again. After Yoku's death, I had clearly heard the ring of truth in a line from Lord Alford Tennyson's poem *In Memoriam A.H.H.,* a meditation on his search for hope after the sudden death of a close friend: "Tis better to have loved and lost than never to have loved at all." However, having nearly drowned in the depths of despair, I didn't yet feel confident enough to risk that dark descent again. I decided I could still enjoy Clara's company but for the time being would play it safe and keep my feelings close to shore.

After our laughter subsided, we settled into a comfortable silence. A good sign, I thought. I've known so many people who compulsively try to fill quiet moments with mindless chatter. I was happy that Clara didn't seem to feel that need.

Airplanes fly us over those places where human density is lowest. And whatever the average human density is in the middle of nowhere, airplanes lower it further by transporting us miles above. Consequently, I experience a deep sense of detachment when flying, and I tend to reflect on where I have been and where I'm going. I found myself thinking back to the last time I visited New Orleans. It was when I was the keynote speaker at a literary festival. Yoku was with me. It was about a year before she died. Instead of flying from Miami we drove, allowing ourselves a few days to explore at a leisurely pace the scenic byways that hug the Gulf coast. It was on that trip that we spent an evening in Apalachicola and when she suggested that I leave the newspaper and we move there. She would probably still be alive if I'd bought into that idea. And, I thought, the two men crushed by a falling pine tree as they drove by would still be alive if their departure had been slightly delayed or extended—a vehicle speeding at 60 miles-per-hour travels over 88 feet in one second—a difference of one tenth of a second either way would have spared their lives. I'd imagined every conceivable scenario in which something I could have done would have changed the course of events leading to Yoku's tragic death. The past, unfortunately, is heartless and immutable, and I eventually stopped obsessing but only after I'd driven myself into a state of physical and emotional exhaustion.

I had been shocked at how Clara seemed to celebrate the death of her husband and thought about asking what originally attracted her to him. It was difficult for me to imagine that there was not anything about him she grieved losing. She spoke before I had a chance to fully form my question. "Gary Coot," she said, with an inscrutable, Cheshire-cat-like smile spreading across her face. Oh Jesus, Goose's cover is blown, I thought.

"What about Gary Coot," I asked?

"Are you really going to pretend you don't know who he is, Eirik, she said sharply."

"I'm not denying that I know him, Clara, I'm asking what *you* know about him," I replied.

"Well, I don't quite know everything about him that I want to know, but I was hoping that you'd fill me in. What I do know for a fact is that he's an ATF agent investigating FLOW. And, given I contribute a lot of money to FLOW, I'd bet he's investigating me too," she said.

I felt ambushed but, trying to remain calm, said that even if it were true that the ATF was investigating FLOW, she should have nothing to worry about unless she was conspiring with them to do something illegal. Before she could react, I implored her to please tell me that she was not. She turned her head away and was quiet for a moment. When she turned back to face me, the smile was gone.

"You of all people know that the river and all the people and wildlife that depend on it are getting screwed. You know that it's all about profits over everything else. And you of all people know that means complete indifference to whatever and whoever gets destroyed. We can't compete dollar-for-dollar with Atlanta's developers and the basin's industrial farmers! Dammit, Eirik,

I'm not willing to stand by anymore and have it forced down my throat that that's just the price of progress," she said angrily.

She was beginning to choke up, and there were tears in her eyes. She was right; I completely understood her anguish and frustration. Most of my life I had pushed against the pillaging of Florida's spectacular natural resources with little obvious effect. However, given her reaction I suspected she was up to no good and I was feeling deeply uncomfortable, I didn't want to be in the position of lying to Clara about what Goose was up to and vice versa. Pulling herself together she confirmed my worst fear saying emphatically, "Listen Eirik, I don't care if I go broke doing it, but I'm going to personally see to it that every dam of any consequence between Apalach and Atlanta is taken down."

In the mid-70s I was heavily under the influence of Edward Abbey's *The Monkey Wrench Gang* and awoke many mornings asking myself whether I should write or blow up a dam. I had taken Abbey's hard-nut hero's job description as my own: "My job is to save the fucking wilderness. I don't know anything else worth saving." Even today among most environmentalists I know, it is an article of faith that blowing up dams would be a good thing primarily because it would reestablish the natural flow upon which entire river ecosystems depend. I agree with John McPhee's description in his 1971 book *Encounters with the Archdruid* of dams as being "disproportionately and metaphysically sinister to conservationists." He speculated that "possibly the reaction to dams is so violent because rivers are the ultimate metaphors of existence, and dams destroy rivers." But however great the environmental angst that dams may provoke, not one of any size in the United States has ever been damaged by an act of eco-tage. There is a good reason for that—it takes a hell of a lot of explosives and demolition knowhow to successfully compromise even a small dam. I suspected that FLOW's dramatic campaign to free the Apalachicola River was designed to first trigger the emotional panic points of the concerned and then demolish their bank accounts. I feared that Clara was being exploited and, if she wasn't careful would end up being implicated in an eco-terrorism conspiracy. I said to her that if FLOW was claiming they were going to blow up even one dam in the basin I thought she was being misled.

"Didn't say a word about blowing anything up *or* doing anything illegal, for that matter, Eirik," she replied coolly.

That was true, but I couldn't help but wonder if she was just trying to cover herself after letting her real intention slip out.

"In fact, FLOW is a perfectly legal 501c3 and I get considerable tax relief from my contributions to them. Now, if they choose to use that money inappropriately that's their little problem, isn't it?" she added.

I couldn't tell her that she was indeed being investigated. But I decided I could tell her about the history of my relationship with Goose and what I knew about AFT surveillance technology and techniques. It was my way of indirectly warning her to be careful about what she said, who she said it to, and where she said it. She looked straight ahead and quietly listened to what I was saying before looking over toward me and giving me what I interpreted to be a look of appreciation.

"I'm going to get a little busy here for a few minutes," she said, "We're beginning our approach to the Lakefront Airport."

It was getting dark and, as I looked down, I could see the headlights of cars on the Pontchartrain Causeway—two parallel bridges 24 miles long that bisect Lake Pontchartrain. It's considered a modern engineering marvel; since the first span was completed in1956 it remains the longest bridge over open water in the world. Covering over 600 square miles, Lake Pontchartrain is not a true lake but the largest inland estuary in the United States. Its south shore borders New Orleans and over many decades its health has been severely compromised by urbanization, industrial activity, levee construction, and the destruction of the wetlands surrounding it. The lake looked beautiful and perfect from the air, but you can't judge the health of an aquatic system by its surface waters alone.

When compared to Lake Pontchartrain, Apalachicola Bay is relatively pristine but I shared Clara's fear that it too would eventually lose out to the relentless pressures of urban development. That thought saddened me, and I turned my attention to Clara who was finalizing our clearance to land. I watched and listened as she expertly moved through a complex set of landing procedures while calmly communicating with the control tower, all of which put to rest any lingering age-related doubts I had about her ability to fly. Upon landing I apologized again for doubting her and said, with as much sparkle as I could still muster in my age-ravaged eyes, that she was clearly an *old* pro. She smiled and accepted my apology in the spirit of which it was intended and gave me a kiss on the cheek. Clara kissed me!

CHAPTER 9

Lake Pontchartrain was out of sight, but I could smell its perfume—a musty, primordial scent. As we walked from the plane toward the terminal building, the voice of Darth Vader emanated from my right coat pocket. "The dark side is calling you," James Earl Jones ominously declared. Gamp had recently taught me how to text photographs and had been playing with the ringtones on my cell. She set up the famous exhortation as my voicemail alert and forgot to show me how to change it. Hoping it might be news regarding my attorney's efforts to recover the money I lost in the Madoff scam, I told Clara that I was expecting a call and would meet her inside. It was Goose reciting a favorite poem of secret agents everywhere. "'Walls have ears. Doors have eyes. Trees have voices. Beasts tell lies. Beware the rain. Beware the snow. Beware the woman you think you know.' New *Awlins* is a mysterious, intoxicating town filled with charm and poetry, Eirik. Be careful my friend. Be very careful." I noted that he said, "the woman you think you know." Catherine Fisher, the author, wrote "the *man* you think you know." No doubt this modification by Goose was intentional and an obvious reference to Clara. It was unsettling to think that possibly our every movement was being followed and every conversation listened to. I tried to assure myself that the New Orleans trip was too spontaneous to have allowed Goose's spooks to bug the plane. Then again, in a post-911 world I thought it would be likely that electronic bugs are antiquated, and listening to a conversation within the cabin of an airplane in flight from a satellite surveillance device or drone might well be possible.

It was the second part of his message, however, that deeply upset me. "Seriously bro, you should know that because of my investigation yesterday, all the components of a 250 pound, small-diameter bomb, except for the explosive charge, were found at an unauthorized site. We think it may have been unexploded ordnance that was spirited out of the Eglin Air Force bombing range. Now get this, the unauthorized site is a Quonset hut way back in the woods less than 100 miles east of the range. Guess the name of the town nearest to the hut. Give up? Remember Wewahitchka? Could be pure coincidence and has nothing to do with FLOW or the Tupelo Alliance, but we're looking into it. The hut was filled with all the tools and electronic gear needed to do surgery on this thing, and it's probable that this isn't the first one that's been worked on. We suspect that they're salvaging parts from multiple duds to build one or more hot ones. Before I hang up, though, here are a few details that might get your attention if I haven't already. These bombs, they're called GBU-39s, are programmable, precision-guided, and were designed to attack, among other things, fixed targets like bunkers. You know, large structures that are kinda engineered like . . .like. . . oh, it's on the tip of my tongue. . .like a DAM. One more thing. An aircraft like your girlfriend's tricked-out ride could easily deliver two of those suckers. Over and out, good buddy."

I have gone through some dramatic changes in my life. All involved turning away from one path I was on and toward another. Some were in reaction to powerful events beyond my control like Yuko's death. Others were the result of my responding to a call from within myself to make a choice, like leaving the *Journal.* Some choices were harder to make than others. Some simplified or made my life easier and some presented me with great challenges or ended up complicating things. Each time I made these moves, my life was altered in profound and often unexpected ways.

While listening to Goose's message I realized he and Clara were on a collision course and that I would not be able to divide my loyalties between them. With what I already knew, should Clara be directly involved in a dam-busting conspiracy (and a single dam was so much as scratched), I could be charged with complicity in a terrorist attack. I felt deeply conflicted. I needed to decide who the hell I was going to side with.

Clara was seated in the back seat of a SUV waiting outside the terminal entrance. As I slipped in beside her, she instructed the driver that she had changed her mind and would like to go to "Kiskatom" before going to dinner at Arnaud's. I'd never heard of Kiskatom and assumed it was a boutique of some kind. Then, turning toward me and resting her hand lightly on my thigh, she said that I looked as though I'd just received some bad news and asked if everything was okay. Before deciding what would happen next in my relationships with Clara and Goose, I wanted to pin Clara down on her level of involvement in what I suspected to be a conspiracy to blow up dams in the ACF basin. However, Goose's voicemail had left me feeling like he could be listening, so instead of taking her question as an opportunity to ask what she was up, to I simply said, "Nothing a stiff drink won't fix."

"Oh my, that bad," she said. "I'm certain that there's a bottle of Freestone's fancy-ass Don Julio tequila I can connect you with. Would that *fix* you up?" I nodded an energetic yes thinking that a bottle of Don Julio *would* fix me up quite nicely. "I'm ready for a Sazerac myself." Speaking to the driver again, she said "Randy dear, would you please call Ta Ta, let her know we're heading her way? Ask her to mix up a pitcher of Sazeracs the special way she does them and check to see if we still have any of Mr. Freestone's favorite tequila left behind the bar."

Kiskatom turned out to be one of thosc stately 19th century homes surrounded by lush gardens that gave the area its name—the Garden District. It was huge, white, and had dark green shutters framing floor to ceiling windows. I guessed it was Greek Revival—fluted columns across the front of the house, real fancy plaster embellishments above the windows and doors, delicate looking ornamental cast iron railings on the upper floor gallery. A dramatic staircase sweeping up from a lush and immaculately landscaped front yard led us to the main entrance on the gallery level where we were greeted by a small, white-haired woman with a ruddy complexion. She and Clara hugged so warmly that at first, I thought she must be a family member. Upon being introduced I learned that Ta Ta had managed the Butterfield's New Orleans home for over forty years. With her arms folded across her chest and her head tilted slightly back, Ta Ta gave me a once over as Clara apologized for giving her such short notice and explained that she just wanted to freshen up and have a drink before going out to dinner. "We'll be out of your hair in no time," she said. As we entered the house, she went on to say that unless the weather deteriorated unexpectedly, we would be flying back to Apalachicola later in the evening. Clara stopped in the foyer and asked Ta Ta to escort me to the library. She then headed up a stairway presumably to "freshen up."

Low-wattage, period-style lighting failed to reach the corners of each room we walked through in the cavernous house, which was filled with antiques and had the formal, hushed ambiance of a museum. I was relieved to discover that the library was well-lighted and smaller. Its furnishings were more contemporary and comfortable looking. Compared to the rest of the house it felt welcoming and intimate. It may have been an actual library at one time, but with a large, wall-mounted TV as the focal point, it looked like it now functioned more like what I would call a media room. As I seated myself at one end of a dark-leather sectional sofa, Ta Ta asked if I'd like my tequila on the rocks or straight up. I said straight up and that I could save her some steps if she just brought me the bottle and a shot glass. She shook her head slowly, sighed, and rolled her eyes before turning and heading out of the room. After what Clara went through with Freestone, I imagined her thinking, "She sure can pick them. Here we go again!"

Thirty minutes later, I heard Clara descend the stairs, walk to an unseen area of the house, and talk briefly to someone (I assumed Ta Ta). I didn't understand anything that was said. Fortified by the bold spirits of tequila, I'd decided to confront Clara on what I believed was a harebrained scheme and confirm her suspicions that she was being investigated by the ATF. My hope was that throwing the weight of my long and tortured history of environmental activism against her heartfelt, but foolish, plan would dissuade her. If that didn't work, maybe learning that she was being spied on by the ATF might scare her away from getting too involved in a conspiracy to commit ecological sabotage.

She entered with a drink in one hand and a book in the other, floated across the room, and in one graceful move lightly seated herself next to me. She looked more attractive than ever. In the space of half an hour she had transformed herself. Casually dressed in beige capri pants and a crisp and cool looking, mint-colored blouse, she exuded an effortless, understated glamour. I absolutely hate how the word is overused but, in this case, it was true; she looked stunning. I felt like a schoolboy struck stupid in the presence of the hottest girl in class. I was greatly relieved when Ta Ta entered with a tray of appetizers, allowing me a moment to start breathing again while I pretended to study the offerings. Clara encouraged me to try Ta Ta's "Panko fried oysters." "She sprinkles them with a blend of Sicilian bottarga, citrus, sun-dried tomato, and a touch of cardamom," she said right before skillfully guiding one into her mouth being careful not to mess up her perfectly applied, brilliant red, lipstick. I was perplexed by how I could be so smitten with someone who couldn't be more different than Yoku, who eschewed any kind of makeup. "And, oh yes, you'll have to try the crab cakes bites with watercress aioli." "The petite crawfish pies are to die for, too." "Damn, they're all exquisite. Try them all," she said happily as she picked up one of the tiny pies and began to lift it to her mouth but stopped short and then gently placed it back down on the tray. Placing her right hand along one side of my face, she hesitated for a moment before leaning forward and kissing me. The kiss was light enough not to disturb her lipstick but long enough to sink my plans to confront her.

Clara, pulled away, looked at me fondly, and said, "You're such a dear man. You remind me of my nephew, Andrew. He died way too soon. We were such great friends. I could trust Andy with my deepest secrets." She turned her head slightly, looking beyond the doorway where Ta Ta had exited, and was silent for a moment. "I'm hoping you and I can learn to trust each other, Eirik." She then handed me a booklet. The cover was an institutional-green color and had no illustrations or photographs that might give me a clue as to its contents. I was shocked when I read the title: *Thiobacillus Thiooxidans: Accelerated Biodegradation of Cement by Sulfur-Oxidizing Bacteria*—concrete eating bacteria.

Being characterized as a "dear man," compared to her nephew, and handed a scientific-looking document on concrete-eating bacteria instantly drained my tequila-flooded libido. Semi-drunk and frustrated, I threw the book down onto the coffee table which then skidded into the tray of hors d'oeurves knocking the tray off the table and onto the floor. Not saying a word Clara calmly looked down at the mess my little tantrum had created and then called to Ta Ta. When Ta Ta entered the room Clara said, "We've had a little accident, Ta." Looking directly at me, Ta Ta said, "I can see that, Ms. Clara; I'll take care of it." We sat in silence while she squatted down, gathered the battered appetizers, and quickly wiped up patches of panko crumb and watercress aioli debris. As she exited the room she glanced over her shoulder and gave me a dark, disapproving look. Goose would have called it "the stink eye." I was embarrassed but not sober enough to have the good sense to apologize.

Spiraling out of control, I abruptly stood up and began flailing my arms around--something I have done since I was a child when upset. “Concrete-eating bacteria? Concrete-eating bacteria? You’ve got to be fucking kidding me, Clara!” Eyes wide and biting her lower lip, Clara looked like she was trying to suppress an urge to laugh. Unsuccessful, she began to laugh so hard that tears began to well up in her eyes.

Through her laughter she managed, “Yes, Eirik, concrete-eating bacteria. CONCRETE-EATING BACTERIA!” She then collapsed backward on the couch holding her belly with one hand and covering her mouth with the other as she tried to stifle her near hysterical laughter. “Oh, merciful god in heaven, help me. Concrete. . . con...crete, . . bacteria,” she whimpered. After catching her breath, she said, “Oh dear, we’ve got to leave now. Arnaud’s doesn’t mess around if you’re late.”

CHAPTER 10

I'm mad as hell and I'm not going to take it anymore, summed up Clara's sentiment toward dams and the Army Corp of Engineers. After she recovered from her fit of laughter and I brought my arms under control, she launched into her rant for why the ACF dams should be taken down: dams block movement of fish and other species, dams change river habitat to pond-like habitat, dams degrade water quality, dams change the flow of the river, dams impact downstream users, and old dams are just disasters waiting to happen. All were key issues that could have been taken verbatim from presentations I'd attended by Endangered Rivers of America, a national environmental advocacy group that focuses on rivers and streams.

Her passionate concern for the fate of the Apalachicola reminded me of myself when I was younger and relished "The Fight" before I gave up all hope of making a difference. Along with many others as angry and determined as myself, I waged hard but futile battles against the ecological decimation of massive portions of undisturbed wilderness in South Florida. However, seeing Clara, eco-warrior, all pumped up and ready to strike rekindled that old flame within me. I considered that getting onboard with her jihad against dams might do me some good. I hated to tell her that compromising the structural integrity of something as massive as a dam with bacteria was probably going to take decades. We'd both be long dead when, and if, it worked. But she probably already knew that. Maybe she felt it was important to do something—anything. Why not, I thought, I didn't have anything left to lose. She wrapped up her tirade with the same cynical conclusion I had come to—that there will never be an equitable plan to share water from the ACF Basin and the Corps will continue to manipulate the water supply to the city of Atlanta's benefit at the expense of everyone else living downstream.

"What is it you'd like me to do," I asked, when at dinner Clara asked if I would help.

"Keep an eye on your ATF friend and feed him a little misinformation from time to time."

"Lie to him," I asked, feeling somewhat incredulous?

"Okay, you don't have to outright lie, just encourage his thinking that someone is planning something a lot more *dramatic* than *concrete-eating bacteria*," she said as she broke into a broad smile and started giggling. I imagined she was remembering my arms failing around like one of those wacky, inflatable tube things you see in used car lots. "Oh, and one other thing," she added, "I want to hire you to help me finish up a writing project I've been working on for years."

"Really, what type of writing project," I asked.

"I guess you'd call it a family history."

"A genealogy?"

"Well, it's not just a family tree, you know, a register-style kind of thing. My grandmother, Maw-Maw, loved to tell stories about life in Apalachicola when she was a girl. I've kept journals almost since I learned to write and whenever there was a story Maw-Maw told that I particularly liked, I entered it from memory as best I could in my journal. When portable tape recorders came along, I started recording her stories as well as those of other elderly family members. I've got stacks of cassettes." I could use the cash I thought, but I had my own writing project that I needed to get started on. I told her I would think about it. She persisted, "We're going to be seeing each other a good bit, you know, on our *special* project. If you were working with me on a book you wouldn't have to lie if your AFT buddy gets curious. I'll draft up a contract, so you'll have some documentation to use as cover should you need to."

She made a good point. I rationalized that telling Goose a half-truth was better than flat out lying. Plus, if the shit hit the fan, it might give me some legal cover. "I don't come cheap," I said half seriously and extended my hand.

She gripped it firmly, and said, "I'm sure you don't but I always get my money's worth." She was dead serious.

"I don't doubt that, I said, but I need more detail before I can make a commitment."

"More detail about what, the writing project or the *demolition* project?" she asked.

"Both," I said, "And before you say anything else, from this point on no matter where we are, we should always assume someone might be listening in. I lowered my voice to a whisper. I don't think you should say *demolition project* again."

She replied in an equally hushed voice, "I wasn't planning to talk to you about *it* again."

"I already know enough to be charged with criminal conspiracy," I said. "Telling me more isn't going to make any difference in how much time I serve."

"Everything you know is purely hypothetical," she said. "The only way you can be charged with conspiracy is if you take some tangible action to further the conspiracy."

"Well, maybe not conspiracy but lying to a federal investigator would classify as obstruction of justice. The Feds consider obstruction to be a felony," I said.

"So, go ahead and tell him the truth, she said. If he asks what the hell I'm up to, tell him I'm planning to dust a dam somewhere in the basin with bacteria—that's all you know so that's all you can tell him. Go ahead, tell him! I guarantee you he'll think I'm a wacko."

I doubted that anyone had ever been arrested for sprinkling bacteria on a dam—the crime would be the intent to destroy the dam. However, I wasn't certain that bacteria would be classified as a destructive force like an explosive device obviously would be. In fact, attacking a dam with bacteria didn't seem to me to be much different from if I were to attack someone with talcum powder while exclaiming that I intended to kill them. In that scenario it's more than likely that I would be taken into custody for psychological evaluation rather than for attempted murder.

I decided I probably *could* tell Goose all I knew and lead him to believe that Clara was delusional and harmless, if he didn't come to that conclusion himself. I certainly was not convinced that a dam could be brought down by accelerating naturally occurring bio-corrosion with bacteria. Maybe she *was* wacko but, delusional or not, I found Clara's fiery desire to strike back exciting. A deep, exhilarating chill rolled up my spine. "Okay," I said as I began to mock myself and flop my arms around, "should he ask me, and only if he asks me, I'll tell him that all I know is that you have this crazy idea about taking down dams with hordes of ravenous, concrete-eating bacteria."

"Oh, my god, what a funny and lovely man you are! How will I keep myself from falling in love with you, Eirik," she interspersed between laughs.

Even though it was well past midnight by the time Clara and I touched down in Apalachicola, I was ready to beat a much-needed retreat from civilization. Even relatively laid-back New Orleans had me feeling fragmented and uptight. It was a moonless night, but I wasn't concerned about finding my way up the river to Owl Creek. I had plenty of candlepower on board The Essex. Candlepower—one rarely hears the word anymore, and I never see it in print. The Egyptians were making candles from beeswax and animal fat 5,000 years ago, and, except for new fuel sources for candles like spermaceti (a wax found in the heads of sperm whales), candles illuminated homes well into the 19th century. In fact, the English defined a single candlepower unit as the light produced by a pure spermaceti candle weighing one sixth of a pound burning at the rate of 120 grains per hour (a grain is about 1/7000 of a pound). A one-candlepower light source is equivalent to a 12.57 lumen light source (a lumen being today's measure of visible light output). As I slowly swept the river channel from one bank to another with my compact 500-lumen, LED "torch," I estimated the 300-ft beam slicing through the darkness was being powered by the equivalent of 6,285 spermaceti candles. I wondered how many sperm whales would have had to die to produce that many candles. The dreadful thought recalled the story of The Essex, my houseboat's namesake.

Spermaceti is what an ill-fated whaling crew was seeking on the morning of November 20 in 1820 when a whale rammed and sunk their ship, The Essex. Having already harpooned two whales from a family of sperm whales they'd been pursuing, the crew observed a whale that was much larger than normal (alleged to be around 85 feet) acting strangely. It lay motionless on the surface with its head facing the ship then began to move toward the vessel, picking up speed by shallow diving. The whale rammed the ship on the port side and then went under, battering it and causing it to rock from side to side. Surfacing close on the starboard side of The Essex with its head by the bow and tail by the stern, the whale appeared to be stunned and motionless. Owen Chase, the first mate, prepared to harpoon it from the deck when he realized that its tail was only inches from the rudder, which the whale could easily destroy if provoked by an attempt to kill it. Fearing to leave the ship stuck hundreds of miles from land with no way to steer it, he relented. The whale recovered and swam several hundred yards ahead of the ship and turned to face the bow. Chase recounted, "I turned around and saw him about one hundred rods (550 yards) directly ahead of us, coming down with twice his ordinary speed, and it appeared with tenfold fury and *vengeance* in his aspect. The surf flew in all directions about him with the continual violent thrashing of his tail. His head about half out of the water, and in that way, he came upon us, and again struck the ship." This blow crushed the bow, driving the 238-ton vessel backwards. Disengaging its head from the shattered bow, the whale swam off as The Essex quickly sank. Taking to three small whaleboats, all 20 members of the crew survived the sinking but with wholly inadequate supplies of food and fresh water, only Owen Chase and seven others lived to tell the tale.

Sperm whales were nearly hunted to extinction in the 1800s and early 1900s. There is no record of a human being eaten by a sperm whale, the largest of toothed, ocean carnivores, and only a handful of reports of "unprovoked" attacks. I named my houseboat The Essex not in honor of the unfortunate crew or the sunken ship, but as a reminder to celebrate that rare moment in history when an individual from a heavily persecuted, non-human species said to itself, "I'm mad as hell and I'm not going to take this anymore," and kicked ass.

By the time I left the grand flow of the lower Apalachicola and entered the more intimate, canopied channel of Owl Creek, I felt I was already falling in love—experiencing a full-body kind of ecstatic sensation tainted only by a pinch of anxiety in my stomach. I was excited about the prospect of a new romantic adventure but couldn't help but fear that, once again, there would be a steep price to pay. I was also exhausted and looking forward to reaching my favorite spot to drop anchor a couple of miles ahead. Entering a sharp bend, I noticed in the sweep of my searchlight that there were a few small boats moored at Hickory Landing (a small, county campground nestled on the eastern bank of Owl Creek), and I slowed to minimize my wake.

As I neared the landing some asshole in the campground began to rapidly flash his automobile's headlights in my direction, switching back and forth from high to low beams. As many local teenagers frequent the park to get drunk or high, I tried to ignore the annoyance until I thought I heard a familiar voice calling my name. It sounded like Gamp. I cut my engine and walked out onto the deck. Still not quite believing my ears, I tentatively called back. "Gamp is that you," I said, as I located a small female figure with my searchlight.

"Yes. We need to talk, Eirik. I tried to catch you before you left Apalach. I guessed you might be heading here. We really need to talk," she said with urgency the second time, "and get that goddam laser beam off me, will you? You trying to set my hair on fire!"

"Okay, sorry," I said, wondering what in the world could be so important that Gamp would track me down at two in the morning. "I'll come on over and you can jump onboard."

"No, no, not onboard, I think your boat might have bugs." she said in a hushed voice. "Throw me a line and I'll tie you off one of these big tupelos. We'll talk in my truck."

Christ, I thought, *that dive of hers probably harbors exotic insect species not yet discovered.* The Essex was as sterile as an operating room compared to the Last Cast.

CHAPTER 11

Gamp's freak out had nothing to do with insects. She wanted to warn me that The Essex might be *bugged* with electronic critters. That night she'd decided to sleep over in her upstairs apartment at the Last Cast and was awakened by a crashing sound followed by a thud. Fearful that I was inebriated and had forgotten to heed her warning about the rotten steps that led down to The Essex's mooring, she hurried downstairs to investigate.

What she found was a heavyset man dressed in black lying face down in the mud bank directly below where he had broken through the rotten step. From her description of the scene, I gathered that the bisected step above where he lay, shaped the Last Cast's mercury vapor lamp light much like "barn doors" do with stage lighting. She said he was perfectly centered in a pool of the distinctive eerie green light. Afraid he would suffocate, she turned over his quivering but unconscious body revealing a black, nylon duffle bag that he had fallen on top of. Suspicious, she quickly unzipped the bag and discovered what she construed to be an assortment of miniature spy gadgets and delicate looking tools and testers like the kind she had seen computer technicians use. Thinking that I might be interested in the bag's contents, she got off a couple of snapshots of the gadgets with her cellphone and a few of the man-in-black as well.

She was uncertain as to whether he was coming from or going to The Essex when he fell. However, concerned that he might be seriously injured, and she might be liable, she called 911. After the emergency medical technicians resuscitated him and determined that he had no broken bones and, despite his stubborn insistence that he was okay, they convinced him he needed to go to the emergency room for a more comprehensive examination and overnight observation. Gamp was taken to the local police station to give her account of the accident. Apparently, it was while she was at the station that I boarded The Essex, never noticing the rotten step that I habitually skipped was gone.

Before 1967 the Fourth Amendment didn't require police to get a warrant to tap conversations over phone lines. That year the Supreme Court made clear that eavesdropping—bugging private conversations or wiretapping phone lines—counted as a search that required a warrant. The Court also said that only police should be allowed to use bugs when investigating serious crimes. Consequently, the Wiretap Act contained a list of crimes deemed "very serious" that could be investigated with a wiretap order. Unfortunately, as the years went by Congress added so many crimes to the list that a warrant could be obtained to wiretap practically anyone suspected of committing or intending to commit a federal offense. Then came the September 11 attacks, and legal restraints on technical surveillance were relaxed to the point that law enforcement can now order wiretaps without a warrant—all in the name of protecting national security.

It was my guess that although I had committed no crime or intended to commit a crime, I had been deemed a person of interest in Goose's investigation simply because of my association with another person of interest—Clara. Together, Clara and I could then be conveniently considered to be *conspiring* to commit a crime. Conspiracy charges make it especially easy for police and federal agents to justify wiretaps. They don't require authorities to prove any actual illegal activity is taking place, only the shared intent.

While covering environmental protests for the *Journal*, I witnessed many of my friends in the Florida environmental community being arrested and charged with a broad range of conspiracy charges for what were just symbolic acts—street theatre. In each case the charges were dismissed on the grounds that the government did not present enough specific information on the alleged criminal activity. One judge's decision read:

> "In order for an indictment to fulfill its constitutional purposes, it must allege facts that sufficiently inform each

> defendant of what it is that he or she is alleged to have done that constitutes a crime. This is particularly important where the species of behavior in question spans a wide spectrum from criminal conduct to constitutionally protected political protest. While 'true threats' enjoy no First Amendment protection, picketing and political protest are at the very core of what is protected by the First Amendment."

I knew that in Clara's mind what she intended *was* direct action and not political protest, but my opinion was that her bacteria "bomb" was so ineffectual that it couldn't be characterized as a true threat. I felt confident that I could convince Goose to see it my way. However, I wasn't at all certain that I could convince Clara to drop her wacky plans to attempt to covertly degrade the ACF dams and opt instead to dust them with her bacteria in well publicized, nonviolent acts of political protest.

I decided I should speak to Clara first but only after The Essex had been swept clean of bugs—the electronic kind. Gamp volunteered the services of her brother's business, Bonsoir Bug. Turns out that Goose's spook never made it past the rotten step—The Essex was bug-free, but Goose was a relentless investigator, and I had no doubt he would persist until he had the intelligence he was seeking. On our New Orleans trip, Clara expressed an interest in coming aboard The Essex and I decided I'd invite her out. She readily accepted my invitation but requested that I meet her at Mile Marker 32—about 10 miles upriver from where Owl Creek joins the Apalach.

You generally find mile markers on rivers used for commercial navigation, and the markers on the Apalachicola originally served barge traffic. In 1946 Congress passed the River and Harbor Act that authorized the Corps of Engineers to maintain a 100-ft wide by 9-ft deep channel in the ACF system from Apalachicola to Columbus, Georgia. For decades thereafter, the Corps dredged and manipulated water levels in the Apalachicola River to keep the river deep enough to float commercial barges hauling bulk commodities like fuel, fertilizer, sand, and gravel. After dredging mountains of sand from the river bottom, the agency disposed of it along the river's banks, in wetlands and the mouths of creeks, damaging the surrounding floodplain forest. The Corp also used its upstream dams to artificially flood the river and then turn off the spigot, devastating populations of river fish and contributing to the decline of valuable commercial fisheries in Apalachicola Bay.

By 2002 the damage was so severe that the Apalachicola was added to a prominent environmental organization's "Most Endangered Rivers List." The destruction was particularly senseless because commercial barge traffic had steadily dwindled due to the Corps' failing about 50% of the time to maintain the 9-ft channel depth the barges required. When pressured in 2000, the Corps disclosed that barge traffic on the river returned only 40 cents to the nation for each federal dollar spent and that barge traffic had dropped to virtually zero. In 2005 the State of Florida got fed up with the Corps, and the Florida Department of Environmental Protection finally shut down their expensive and destructive practices by denying a request to continue dredging the river bottom.

Studying my map, I noted there was a long and uncharacteristically straight stretch of the normally winding river that began around mile maker 32. As I exited Owl Creek and turned upstream, I wondered why Clara would choose to meet me by boat at a location over thirty miles from her home rather than make the shorter and quicker drive to Hickory Landing where Gamp had flagged me down. Our rendezvous point was certainly more remote than the landing but most of the river flows through an equally remote and largely unpopulated floodplain. If, when exiting Owl Creek, I turned downstream, back toward Apalachicola, I would more than likely have encountered recreational boaters—where I was heading is too wild to be popular with them. I do see fishermen on the upper part of the river but generally they are in route to the smaller, fish-rich tributaries of the Apalach. At mile marker 32 I had yet to see a single soul as I dropped anchor. Given the exquisite absence of all mechanical noise that morning, I expected the drone of her boat's engine would announce her arrival long before she came into view. I made myself a cup of tea, settled into a chair on the upper deck, and waited.

A few minutes later I heard a motor, but it didn't sound like an outboard—more like the distinctive high-revving pitch of a personal watercraft. Judging from the rate at which the sound was building in intensity, I guessed it was really hauling butt and would soon come around the bend and out into the straight stretch of the river where I was anchored. Fully expecting to see a boat of some kind, I was completely taken by surprise when a small, silver-blue airplane banking hard (one wingtip practically skimming the surface of the river) whipped around the bend. It quickly leveled out and waggled it wings as it flew directly over The Essex. I watched it gain altitude as it continued upriver before going into a wide and graceful turn. Once heading down river, the pilot lowered the nose of the plane and throttled down as though preparing to land. Seeing nothing but two stubby looking struts where the landing gear should be, I became alarmed thinking that the wheels had somehow been sheared off and he might be attempting an emergency water landing.

Assuming the worst, I scrambled down the stairs to the lower deck just as the plane glided past at eye-level. Clara, alone in the sleek, tinted canopy looked over and smiled as she "landed" what I realized was an amphibious plane. The two "stubs" were hydrofoils that held the fuselage above the water during the higher speed, and potentially damaging, early stage of landing. It was an elegant little aircraft with the aerodynamic, sweeping lines of a sailplane. Upon landing Clara turned around, slowly cruised upriver until parallel with The Essex, and shut down the single, tail-mounted engine. Simultaneously the canopy lifted upward and forward in one fluid motion. Clara stood in the now open cockpit and expertly threw a mooring line to me over the short stretch of water separating The Essex and her plane. I gently pulled the plane over to the aft deck. Stepping out onto a step integrated into one of the hydrofoils, she extended her hand for assistance saying, “Permission to come aboard, Captain Nilsson?” I took her hand replying, “Permission granted, Ms. Butterfield.” First she removed her shoes—a common boarding courtesy in the yachting world where teak decks can be dented or scuffed by hard soled shoes. It was a sweet gesture, but The Essex was decked with heavy aluminum plate and impervious to damage by anything other than an oxyacetylene cutting torch.

Clara’s feet were petite and her toenails perfectly manicured, unlike my hairy hooves with fungus-thickened and -discolored nails. I was certain she would be horrified if she ever saw them. I was unaware of how long I had been staring at her immaculate dogs when she began to wiggle her toes. Snapping my head upward, I squeezed out,

“Beautiful feet. Would you care for something to drink?

“If it’s not too much trouble, Eirik, I’d love a cup of tea.”

I entered The Essex and headed across the living area to the galley. "Please make yourself comfortable, Clara, I just made a pot of Keemun."'

"Really, Keemun, she said as she settled onto the sofa."

"You're familiar with Keemun?"

"Only the Hao Ya variety—Freestone bought pounds of it directly from a grower in China."

"I can't begin to imagine how much that would cost," I said.

"I told you he had expensive taste," she said with a hint of bitterness in her voice.

"Milk? Sugar?"

"I like it straight up, Chinese style," she replied.

Before Madoff, that whoreson, gorbellied, nut-hook, ripped me off, I could justify paying $60 to $70 per pound for Keemun Hao Ya. A pound would generally yield about 150 cups—40 to 50 cents per cup. At twice the price Keemun would still be a bargain in my mind when compared to a Coke or the cup of generic black tea you get in a typical café or restaurant. I was getting down to seeds and stems and I wondered if Clara had any of Freestone's stash left. "Are you a fan of Keemun?" I asked.

"I like it, but I generally drink green teas." We were both silent for a moment while I prepared her cup and refreshed mine.

Legs crossed, and hands folded in her lap, she seemed immersed in thought before speaking again, "You're welcome to whatever Keemun is left at the house, Eirik. I won't be using it." As much as I wanted to accept, I habitually ceded to my upbringing which informed me that to jump on her offer would seem opportunistic and rude. Instead, I thanked her for her generosity and made a counteroffer to pay for it. "Pay me for it? Are you trying to insult me Eirik? Didn't your mother teach you how to accept a gift graciously? Besides, you obviously love that stuff. I know you want it badly," she said with a broad smile. I enjoyed her poking fun at my transparent attempt at modesty.

"Feel free to insult me, Miss Clara, I shot back with mock indignation, but I will not tolerate your sullying my dead mother's fine reputation." She laughed heartily. "I was enjoying the morning air on the upper deck when you arrived," I said as I gestured to spiral staircase on the aft deck. "Care to have our tea up there?"

"Yes," she said, and even though I enjoy small talk I'm curious to know what's really on your mind."

"Of course, I said, but before we get to that tell me all about that exquisite little plane of yours."

"She *is* quite a pearl, isn't she," she said enthusiastically as we headed upstairs. "Let's see: French-made, carbon composite airframe, you saw the hydrofoils and the electric canopy in action, also has retractable landing gear for runway landings with optional skis for landing on snow, wings fold back for storing or hauling around on the back of a yacht, 100 horse engine that runs on unleaded gas and gets 36 miles-per-gallon at 118 miles per hour, cruising speed is 133, top speed of 155, climbs 1400 feet per minute, range is close to 1000 miles, takes off and lands in less than 700 feet, seats two side-by-side, dual controls, great avionics."

"It was designed purely for recreational purposes, right?" I asked as we seated ourselves.

She replied sharply, "What are you suggesting?" I had touched a nerve.

"I'm not suggesting anything, I said, I only meant that it's like the flying equivalent of an ATV or personal watercraft—an expensive toy."

"I see, she said, I thought maybe you were thinking that I was planning to use it like a crop duster for spraying bacteria over dams."

"No, that's not at all what I was thinking but now that you've brought it up that's what I wanted to talk to you about—the bacteria thing."

"What about it?" she said tersely.

"Well, first, I don't think it's going to work and is therefore definitely not worth risking going to prison for. I *do* think it would be better for the Apalach if you used the bacteria in a symbolic way."

"What do you mean, symbolic?"

"I mean use it in an obviously theatrical way to draw the public's attention to the plight of the river."

"Okay then, she said brightening up, "if that's what you think I should do then that's what I'll do." For days I had dreaded having this conversation with Clara and tried to prepare myself for a heated and protracted argument. I had feared that she would stubbornly reject anything that contradicted her plan and perhaps reject me too. I *was not* prepared for such easy acquiescence—too easy.

"That's it?" I asked.

"Not quite," she said, I know nothing about how to go about environmental theatre. You're the old activist. I'm new to this game—I'll need your help."

I was still unconvinced but felt relieved that at least she appeared to be moving in a direction I was more comfortable with. "I've participated in protests and as a journalist I covered protests, but I don't have any experience organizing them. However, I can hook you up with some people who would be delighted to help us out," I said.

"Perfect. You know Eirik, staging these things and working on my book means we're going to be spending a lot of time together. My friend has moved out of the farmhouse. You're welcome to move in. It has a dock; you could moor The Essex there. I also have a security guard on the property 24/7—no need to worry about your *friend,* Agent Coot, *bugging* you."

I immediately wanted to say yes but once again buckled under the rules of polite behavior. "I don't believe that I can afford to rent a toothbrush," I said.

"You know I mean move in as a guest, Eirik—as *my* guest," she said with a twinkle in her eye. *Who is pursuing whom,* I wondered?

Before I could say yes, she asked, "Are you hesitant because of Yoku?" I was stunned to hear Clara speak her name—it evoked a vivid image of Yoku from my memory. I was speechless. She continued, "I've gathered that there's been no other woman in your life since she died. You must have loved her very much. It's only natural for you to feel conflicted about our budding . . . friendship, you know." *So, the feeling is mutual,* I thought. "I know a thing or two about losing loved ones, but the finish line is drawing closer for both of us, especially me. I'll respect your feelings for Yoku, Eirik, but my gut tells me that maybe you have room in your heart for someone new. Am I wrong?"

CHAPTER 12

"Eirik, you know as well as I do that if you lie down with dogs, you'll get up with fleas," Goose said in response to my question about his attempt to bug The Essex. "That woman is playing you for a fool and she may be hazardous to your health too; two of her three husbands died under suspicious circumstances!" Getting a little worked up by Goose's assault on Clara, I challenged him to explain to me how she rigged up getting Freestone to drive into the path of a freight train. "Maybe he wasn't driving at all. No one saw him racing the train. One witness who came on the scene right after it happened claimed that even though the guy was as flat as a road-kill-frog, there was extraordinarily little blood. That would incline a rational person to suspect that he was dead before that locomotive hit him."

"Was she charged, I asked?"

"No, he answered, but you should know that everyone in this town is on her payroll or has been at one time or another. The Butterfield family has been like a dynasty in Franklin County since the mid-1800s. She's president of this and that civic organization, owns multiple businesses including the biggest bank in town, she's endowed a foundation that's sent dozens of kids through college, she even fronts the oystermen money right out of her pocket when times get tough; everyone around here owes her something."

"Well fuck, Goose, I said angrily, that sure is some dangerous sounding shit."

"Spare me the obscenities Eirik; I'm just saying she's got enough influence around here to shape things in her favor however she wants to. She also began moving a lot of money out of the country starting a few months ago."

"Is that illegal, I asked, don't thousands of people do that all the time?"

"No, it's not illegal but it darn sure is suspicious when someone with virtually no history of depositing money offshore suddenly begins transferring millions to a Belizean bank, don't you think?"

"I don't know what to think about that, Goose," I practically shouted. "I lost my ass trusting a "highly respected" investment advisor, maybe my money *would* have been better off in an offshore account. You know what I think, Goose? I think you've been at this spook game for too long. You're paranoid! Do you remember warning me that I should use my credit card more instead of paying cash all the time because the FBI considers that to be a potential indicator of terrorist activity? And that whole thing about profiling people WITHOUT Facebook accounts as potential psychopaths; do you realize how screwed up that is?"

Goose was on fire. "Eirik, I can't protect you! I can't look the other way! I can only warn you that Clara Butterfield is not who you think she is and that you shouldn't trust her in the least! From this point on, you are on your own my friend," he said, the cutaneous veins in his neck bulging with anger and frustration as he stomped off The Essex and up the dilapidated stairway toward Water Street and the Last Cast.

Goose and I had our share of heated arguments in the past, but I had never seen him so upset, and I felt bad that I'd lost it with him. I decided I should apologize, but as I got to my feet he had already turned around and was heading back to The Essex. We stood facing each other for a moment. He began to speak but I interrupted him saying that I was sorry for what I'd said about him being paranoid, that I knew he was only trying to look out for me, and that I appreciated his concern. He said there was some truth to what I said about his being overly suspicious, but he would never be able to forgive himself if he didn't give me the information I needed to at least make an intelligent decision. I thanked him and said I considered him to be a good friend. We had both calmed down by then, and I offered him a drink.

He accepted and as he seated himself, he said, "I know, Eirik, that I probably can't dissuade you from seeing more of Clara Butterfield, but if FLOW is up to what I think they're up to, then we're talking about something deadly serious that you need to know about. Are you at least willing to listen to what I have to say?"

"Of course, I said, but first I'd like to hear to what end you think Clara would be using me."

"My theory is that she's using you as a shield—that I'll hesitate to investigate her knowing you might also get caught in it," he replied.

"She doesn't know you very well, does she," I said.

"No," he said, "but I must admit I'm being more cautious than usual so if that's her strategy, it's working. Considering the possible consequences for you *are* distracting me. Now, I've got a question for you."

"Shoot," I said.

"Why do you think it was so easy for her to let go of the bacteria idea?"

"I'm not sure," I replied, "but I'm assuming because it was never a serious consideration."

"That's what I think too. What I do find suspicious, though, is when and how she chose to print out that document she shared with you. It was the same day we discovered the bunker bomb shop in WeWa."

“I don’t follow,” I said.

“I think it was intended to be a red herring. She could have printed it at home, but she chose the public library instead and left a duplicate in the trash can. She knows we’re watching her closely. It was like she wanted us to find it.”

“You mean you still think she has a hand in the bomb shop,” I said.

“We don’t have any evidence to support that, but I haven’t ruled out her involvement.”

“But Goose,” I said, the concrete-eating bacteria thing would only work as a red herring if it were a credible threat. I mean, even I know that destroying a major dam with bacteria is a ludicrous idea.”

“Not if the bacteria are weaponized; the Army’s been working on a super strain. But, yes, it’s a stretch even for someone as paranoid as me to believe that she was serious. Maybe she just wanted me to shift my focus at that moment, you know, like she threw a feint. As I said, it was her timing more than anything else that made me suspicious.”

Seeing my look of incredulity, he changed the subject. “Okay, moving right along, my guys have worked hard on this, and I think you’ll find it interesting. Make yourself comfortable, this is going to take a while for me to lay it all out for you. Just bear with me. It starts with Buford Dam. Buford Dam impounds Lake Lanier, which has a storage volume of about 637 billion gallons of water or 86 billion cubic feet. The Superdome has an interior space of 125 million cubic feet. We're talking close to 750,000 Superdomes full of water here—a shitload of water!" I was surprised—Goose rarely cursed. "Between Buford Dam, just north of Atlanta, and Jim Woodruff dam, on the Florida-Georgia border, which you know is where the Flint and the Chattahoochee converge to form the Apalachicola River, there are 13 other dams in the Chattahoochee River corridor—a few major ones but mostly smaller dams. The distance between Buford and Woodruff is a little over 300 miles—but has a chain of 15 dams. Like a chain, a multi-dam water management system is only as strong as its weakest link, and when the weakest link is far upstream, the downstream risk is magnified."

"How so," I asked.

"Glad you asked," he said, "Catastrophic cascade failure is what they call it. A single dam failure far upstream can start a domino effect by the sudden release of a massive volume of water that takes out a second dam releasing even more water, and so on."

"Aren't dams designed to deal with huge volumes of water like during floods," I asked?

"Yes, they're designed to handle the slow buildup of water from rainfall, but there's not a dam on the Chattahoochee engineered to withstand the speed or the pressure of hundreds of billions of gallons of water coming at it all at once. Plus, over time the catchment areas behind dams accumulate debris and silt which would also be released, and the rush of water and debris would scour the riverbanks and pick up even more debris as it progressed downstream. In floods it is usually the debris, not the water that does the most damage."

"Let me paint the rest of the picture for you now: Someone waits until a hurricane or tropical storm moves up through Florida and into Georgia bringing the four biggest reservoirs on the Chattahoochee up to full pool with Lanier brimming over with 637 billion gallons, West Point Lake close to 200 billion, Lake George 300 billion, and Seminole 120 billion. At that point, the stage is set for the most destructive and deadly act of ecotage in American history. Now, imagine two or three men under the cover of darkness positioning a military-grade bomb, just like that 250-pound GBU-39 we discovered in Wewa, underwater at the upstream base of the dam and then exploding it. The explosion forces a separation between the earthen dam and tons of water. The mass of water retreats around the expanding blast bubble and then slams back into the dam, excavating a hole."

"Wait a second, I said, Buford Dam is a dirt dam, not concrete?"

"Yes, it's a rolled-fill earth type of dam; layers upon layers of compacted earth—some rock and clay in there but mostly dirt. The powerhouse is reinforced concrete and steel, but the dam and saddle dikes are dirt. Surprised?" I nodded that I was. Goose continued. "Layers of earth are forced out of the way as the corrosive avalanche of water and silt erodes the original blast hole until it is a rapidly expanding chasm in the wall of the dam. Then, the dam's downstream wall ruptures, and, in a raging torrent, Lanier's billions of gallons of water begin to barrel toward metro Atlanta."

As Goose speaks, I'm thinking that the great irony here is that Buford Dam was originally built to protect Atlanta from the Chattahoochee's seasonal flooding. Atlanta was originally sited on the crest of large ridge, but over the decades the rapidly growing city spilled over into the floodplain.

"Within minutes the first word of the dam break begins to reach the public. Panic ensues as media and emergency rescue teams try to alert everyone living downstream. The municipalities of Suwanee, Norcross, and Marietta are quickly and completely inundated before the destructive mass of water and debris erases the affluent town of Vinings that sits directly in its path. The death toll begins to mount. Less than three hours later Lanier's waters collide with the headwaters of West Point Lake. West Point Dam is a large dam, but its 200-billion-gallon capacity cannot restrain the sudden introduction of the additional billions of gallons, and it fails. The wall of destruction then continues to roar down the basin, destroying dam after dam, ripping a path of death and destruction all the way to the Gulf of Mexico.

Starting with a single explosion, hundreds of thousands of people are affected; thousands of businesses and homes are destroyed; food supply systems, water supply systems, and sewer systems are damaged or destroyed, and it will take billions of dollars and years to restore them. Think about it, Eirik; one bomb, one single act of destruction timed just right and . . ." Goose gravely shook his head before sipping his drink.

I didn't know how to respond. The concept of cascading dam failures had never entered my mind. My first reaction was to strongly doubt that even the most radical eco-terrorist group would scheme to unleash the horror that Goose had so dramatically illustrated for me. It was easy to imagine jihadists conducting such an attack, but every direct-action environmental group I knew of followed a code of non-violence toward all living creatures. I asked Goose why he suspected that FLOW had anything to do with the bomb shop and not a group like al-Qaeda.

"We haven't ruled out Islamic militants; we just don't have any solid evidence that they're operating in this region. One reason FLOW is in our crosshairs is that we were tipped off by a local that he'd seen some "hippie, environmentalist types" coming and going from that hut at odd hours of the night. That's what led us to investigate what was going on there in the first place. Plus, there's the obvious: FLOW has clearly stated that their reason for being is to "liberate" dams, and they are affiliated with a direct-action group responsible for hundreds of thousands of dollars in damages. So tell me, given the same information would you conclude that it is purely coincidental that someone is rehabilitating military grade ordinance capable of blowing a hole in a dam? Oh, before you answer that question, throw into the mix a local individual with very deep pockets who is sympathetic to their cause to the tune of many thousands of dollars."

"There's nothing illegal about Clara's donations to FLOW Goose," I said.

"And, as long as she doesn't get herself involved any deeper than that. I can't touch her, Eirik," Goose replied, "but she's in deep enough already for me to keep my eyes on her." Then after a dramatic pause he said in an exaggerated Italian accent, "Capiche?" I cracked up. Capiche was our private joke. I was investigating a story at the *Times* about a small-time Miami drug dealer who fancied himself to be Don Vito Corleone. He wasn't even Italian. Goose brought him down and when under interrogation he'd end every other hilarious explanation for why he wasn't guilty with, "Capiche?" I enjoyed Goose's sense of humor and his friendship. I laughed and said in a mock-serious tone, "Capiche."

I felt relieved that Goose and I had straightened things out. By the time I got around to telling him I was going to accept Clara's invitation to move into her guest house, he seemed to take it all in stride. I guess he had said his piece and had decided to leave it at that. I didn't buy anything he had to say about Clara, but I'd always known him to have good instincts and I knew that I wouldn't be able to completely put aside his suspicions. No matter what he thought, I felt it would probably be a good idea anyway to go into a relationship with Clara with my eyes wide open. Soon after Goose headed out, I went up to the Last Cast to celebrate my decision to accept Clara's invitation and move into the Japanese farmhouse with a few shots and settle my bar tab with Gamp. It was at that moment that I realized I hadn't associated drinking with anything as bright as a celebration in far too many dark years.

CHAPTER 13

It had been two months since I'd moved into Freestone's "folly," as Clara often referred to the ancient farmhouse on the river, and we had settled into a comfortable routine—dinners most days up at the main house and breakfasts at the farmhouse. In between, when she was not off meeting with one or another of the various organizations she was involved in or I wasn't writing, we'd get together. It wasn't important to us that our relationship have any particular pattern, it had just shaped itself around our individual and common interests.

Watching classic movies was one common interest, and we periodically flew to N.O. for the classic films featured every Sunday and Wednesday at the Prytania Theatre. Opened in 1915 and having survived fires, hurricanes, and mega-movie complexes, it is the oldest theatre operating in New Orleans and the only single-screen theatre in the state of Louisiana. I found it personally inspiring that the Prytania had defied wind, fire, and sweeping changes in the movie industry, but the icing on cake was the completely charming Rene Brunet, the 90-year-old owner and epitome of human optimism and resilience, who would take the stage to introduce the priceless old flicks with great panache.

It was during a showing of the original *Cat on a Hot Tin Roof* with Elizabeth Taylor and Paul Newman that Clara first slipped her hand into mine. The scene was where Maggie, sensual but deprived, describes her passionate feelings for her husband Brick, who will not so much as touch her.

> Maggie: "Why can't you lose your good looks, Brick? Most drinkin' men lose theirs. Why can't you? I think you've even gotten better lookin' since you went on the bottle." (As she caresses the brass bedframe) "You were such a wonderful lover...You were so excitin' to be in love with. Mostly, I guess, 'cause you were" (pause)..." If I thought you'd never never make love to me again" (pause)" ...why I'd find me the longest, sharpest knife I could, and I'd stick it straight into my heart. I'd do that. Oh Brick, how long does this have to go on?"

Maybe Clara's timing was purely coincidental, but I couldn't help but wonder if it was something in that scene that moved her to reach out to me. She didn't know me before I "went on the bottle" so I know it didn't have anything to do with that line. Plus, I knew for a fact that drinking hadn't done anything to improve my looks unless you considered the spider angiomas on my face irresistible. Susceptible to over analyzing everything, I decided to try to relax and enjoy the heart-connected intimacy of holding hands in the darkness of a movie theater.

Later that evening on the sofa at her Garden District home, we held each other momentarily and exchanged a few shy, delicate kisses, whereupon she stood, hugged me warmly, thanked me for a lovely evening, and proceeded to her upstairs bedroom. I enjoyed our "dates," but despite my strong attraction to her, I once again found myself filled with feelings of guilt and betrayal with each new intimacy. I was beginning to think I'd misjudged my readiness to swim in deeper emotional waters. As I lay in bed in the carriage house apartment where I slept on our movie nights, I desperately wanted to talk to Yoku. Besides being my wife, she had also been my best friend and confidant, and I yearned for her always sage advice. I wondered if I would ever be able to get close to Clara without feeling guilty.

We had just finished breakfast at the farmhouse one morning when Clara, while folding her napkin with what I thought was exaggerated care, looked up and said, "I think it's time you and I have a talk about sex." Not believing that she could be serious, I jokingly asked her what it was that she would like to know. She smiled, but the look in her eyes told me she was serious.

"Oh," I said, "we're really going to have this discussion."

"Maybe I should rephrase that," she said, I think it's time I tell you how *I* feel about sex if you're interested in listening." I felt slightly relieved. I told her she had my complete attention. "I don't know what you know about women my age, Eirik, so I'll assume not much. Some of us don't feel sexual desire the way we use to. I'm one of those women. That's not to say that I can't become . . ." She squirmed in her chair a bit, turned away from me slightly, and looked out across the river. I thought I saw a slight blush rise in her cheeks. ". . . *aroused* or even have an orgasm, I'm just saying that I don't have that old. . . *itch*. ... anymore." She looked back at me and continued to speak. "It's not that I don't find you attractive or sexy. I do. I'm just saying that at this point in my life I don't do anything if I don't *feel* like doing it, and that includes sex." She then reached out her hand to me across the dining table and as I took it in mine she said, "I hope, my dear friend, you can accept that and won't take it personally if I'm not interested in hopping into bed with you."

Aside from her elegant countenance that initially captured my attention, it was Clara's strong character and startlingly directness that continued to fuel my fascination with her. Until she disclosed her feelings about her sexuality, she had shared little about herself. Her sudden openness about something so intimate took me by surprise. I saw a look of vulnerability in her eyes that I hadn't seen before. Yoku believed that meaningful, intimate relationships start when someone dares to be genuine—that there was power in vulnerability. I thought what Clara had done was courageous and I also read it as an invitation to open myself to the possibility of a deeper and more emotionally intimate relationship with her.

After Yoku's death I slid into a world where security meant solitude and emotional connection meant the potential for great suffering. Now, for the first time since losing her I was being presented with an opportunity to break out of that lonely place. I recalled Yoku patiently trying to reeducate me, "Eirik, listen to me, you need to learn this. Vulnerability is not weakness; it is the birthplace of love, belonging, and creativity. It is the source of empathy and authenticity. If you want a more meaningful life, vulnerability is the path." I was scared. I wasn't certain I could risk again waking up every day loving someone who may or may not love me back, whose safety I couldn't ensure, who may stay in my life or leave (or die) at a moment's notice, who may be loyal to the day they die or betray me tomorrow. On the other hand, life without loving someone, and being loved, was cold and colorless, so I did what I hoped Yoku would want me to do.

I held Clara's hand firmly and said, "When I was younger, I wouldn't ever have imagined that I'd feel this way, but given the choice between sex and a close friendship with someone like you, I'd give up sex."

She straightened up in her chair and studied me for a moment before saying, "Seriously, you'd give up sex just like that? T.D.?"

"T-what," I asked.

"T.D.," she repeated, "Tequila dick, a condition Freestone developed." Her crude assertion inserted into what I thought was a tender and intimate moment stunned me, and it took a few seconds for me to understand that she was alluding to erectile dysfunction; alcohol-induced ED—tequila dick. I felt insulted. I was still capable of hoisting a perfectly respectable hard-on, and it also seemed she was equating my drinking behavior with Freestone's wild, drug- and alcohol-fueled benders. The fact of the matter was that since I'd moved into the farmhouse and was seeing Clara on a regular basis, I'd been drinking a whole lot less. I jerked my hand away from hers.

She reacted with surprise and blurted, "Eirik, I was just teasing, lighten up. There's no shame in getting older; we have to keep our sense of humor about these things—saggage and shrinkage happens!"

She was laughing that infectious laugh of hers as she stood up and walked over to my side of the table. While I was still seated, she embraced me from behind. Leaning over and kissing me on the side of my face she said in a soft and gentle voice, "I didn't mean to be rude. It's just that you were getting so serious I couldn't resist poking a little fun at you. It's not so stark a choice as you make it out to be. Good lord, we're not young and randy, but we're certainly not dead yet. I was just trying to lower your expectations in case you were all . . . hot-to-trot."

I felt over-reactive and embarrassed, but her hug and assurances helped me quickly find my own sense of humor. "Really," I said, "hot-to-trot—how old ARE you?"

"Actually, hot-to-trot wasn't what came to my mind first. It was what I thought was the better choice after hot-and-bothered and in-the-mood," she said with a straight face. "Would you have preferred horny?"

"I think people still say horny in the 21st century," I said.

She kissed me again before straightening up and said that she had an appointment in Chattahoochee she needed to get to. As she walked toward the door, she added that she wanted to talk about forming an Apalachicola River environmental action committee when she returned.

"I would love to, but I'm taking The Essex upriver for a couple of nights. I may not be here when you return," I said.

"Oh, okay, that's fine; we'll talk when you return. Enjoy," she said over her shoulder as she continued to walk.

"Google West Marin EAC," I shouted just before the door closed behind her. The West Marin environmental action committee was one of the country's oldest. It began as a grassroots advocacy group dedicated to protecting the spectacular and priceless natural resources of a wild coastal region of Marin County, California commonly referred to as West Marin. Like the Apalachicola River Basin West Marin is primarily rural, and its small communities lacked the resources to monitor, much less act against, threats to the natural environment.

It had been too many weeks since I had had any time alone. People often confuse being alone with being lonely—I don't. After Yoku died I suffered a great deal of loneliness. Loneliness has a deep ache to it and feels more like being adrift in dark and unfamiliar waters. Solitude is intentional and can have purpose. As a teenager I would periodically slip off to a favorite spot on a remote stretch of a beach not far from home and just sit and think. I generally returned home from those solitary experiences feeling refreshed and renewed. As I matured, I came to recognize that if I ignored my need for solitude, I lost that comforting sense of having a clear perspective gained from quiet contemplation, and I'd soon find myself being driven by lists, schedules, and the petty concerns of contemporary social life.

As I left the farmhouse, I impulsively grabbed my well-worn copy of Joan Didion's *The Year of Magical Thinking* in which she meticulously documents the occurrences and aftermath of the sudden death of her partner of 40 years and simultaneous life-threatening illness of their only child. It was published not long after Yoku died, and I was immediately drawn into her story by the blurb on the dust jacket:

> "This powerful book is Didion's attempt to make sense of the 'weeks and months that cut loose any fixed idea I ever had about death, about illness . . . about marriage and children and memory . . . about the shallowness of sanity, about life itself."

"The shallowness of sanity" set the hook. I found myself reading one scene in her story again and again. In it she faces gathering and giving away her husband's clothing. Each article of his clothing stirs up memories as she places it in a bag that she will eventually deliver to a nearby church. The process is painful, and weeks pass by before she can return to the task. Eventually, she feels prepared to deal with his shoes. She stops at the door to the room where the shoes are stored. She can't enter the room. She can't give his shoes away. Standing there she realizes why she can't—he would need them if he were to return. This is the beginning of her realization that she isn't thinking rationally.

Far upriver and finally ensconced in solitude, I once again read the sections of Didion's book that I found most compelling and considered for the first time whether I was, figuratively speaking, not able to give Yoku's shoes away. Was I, I wondered, like Joan Didion, holding on to the irrational notion that someday Yoku would return? Was I trying to keep her alive?

Why else would I feel guilty for being disloyal if not because I had not come to grips with her "unending absence?" In her closing Didion addresses the question of why we try to keep the dead alive. "We try to keep them alive in order to keep them with us," she flatly answers. At some point we must "relinquish the dead" and ". . . let them go, keep them dead," she says solemnly.

Before meeting Clara, each time I came to this point in *The Year of Magical Thinking* I would rationalize that it's easy to say or write such things or, that we all grieve differently or, I would doubt that Joan Didion could have loved her husband as deeply as I did Yoku; otherwise, she would have found it impossible to keep the love of her life "dead." However, as I sat out on the deck of The Essex, attempting to untangle my knotted thoughts and emotions, it became clear to me that keeping Yoku's memory alive created a huge conflict for me in my relationship with Clara and that it was evolving into a macabre, torn-between-two-lovers kind of conundrum. To resolve this issue, I was going to have to remain married for the rest of my life to the memory of a dead lover or "relinquish the dead" and give my heart to someone very much alive.

No other part of the nation has more thunderstorm activity than Florida. The frequency of summer thunderstorms in some parts of Florida equals that of the world's maximum thunderstorm areas like the Lake Victoria region of equatorial Africa and the middle of the Amazon basin. But the sound that awoke me from a deep sleep later that evening was unlike any thunder I've heard—more like a singular, hard thump rather than a rumbling sound. I was almost certain I felt The Essex vibrate before hearing anything.

Lighting creates a sudden increase in pressure and temperature and causes the surrounding air to expand violently at a rate faster than the speed of sound, like a sonic boom. The shock wave extends outward for the first 30 feet or so, after which it becomes an ordinary sound wave called thunder. Thunder is just the result of exploding air occurring along the entire length of the lightning channel. The sound of distant thunder has a characteristic low-pitched rumbling sound. Pitch, the degree of highness or lowness of a sound, is due to strong absorption and scattering of the high-frequency components of the original sound waves, while the rumbling results from the fact that sound waves are emitted from different locations along the lightning channel, which lie at varying distances from a person. The longer the lightning channels, the longer the sound of thunder.

Moving up to the deck, I could see a pinkish glow in the cloudless night sky over about where Apalachicola would be. As far upriver as I was, I typically didn't see any light pollution emanating from the small town. I presumed the source was a fire—a rather large one at that. Half asleep and not curious enough to wake Gamp in the middle of the night, I returned to bed thinking I would give her a call in the morning.

CHAPTER 14

Millions of Americans have vivid memories of traumatic public events, events like John F. Kennedy's assassination, the Challenger space shuttle explosion and, more recently, the 9/11 attacks. Psychologists characterize these remembrances as "flashbulb memories;" detailed recollections as clear as something that happened yesterday, right down to smells, sounds, weather, and even what people were wearing when they heard the news. The memories are so emotionally powerful that they are etched in their minds as vividly, completely, and accurately as a photograph. I know this is true from my own experience with great public tragedies. I also know that this phenomenon is true for less public, deeply personal misfortunes. The moment I learned Yoku was dead is certainly permanently seared into my memory.

More and more flecks of color were appearing in the forest. A blanket of fog lay low on the river as I went about my morning ritual. I boiled water for tea, turned the heat off on a small pot of grits, and then poached a couple of eggs. As the sun's warmth was drying the last droplets of dew from the tall grasses along the water's edge,

I took my second cup of tea on the upper deck. Later, as I was standing at The Essex's galley sink cleaning dishes, I paused to watch a mother duck with what appeared to be ducklings on her back, staying in close to the riverbank and heading downstream at a pretty good clip. I wondered if she was attempting to elude some unseen predator when my phone rang. It was Gamp. I immediately asked if she knew anything about what sounded like an explosion in the middle of the night. Gamp's extensive network of friends and family made her a valuable resource when I wanted to get the inside story on just about anything going on in town and up and down the river. I had no doubt that she would have already gathered a lot of juicy information.

The actual moment when hope ceased to exist for me didn't of itself bring its death; it had been a long time coming and was merely the straw that broke the proverbial camel's back. That moment was when I learned from Gamp that Clara had *disappeared.* As told to Gamp by her brother-in-law, a Franklin County deputy sheriff, ATF agents arrived at Clara's with the intent to serve her with a search warrant when someone in the 300-year-old Japanese farmhouse fired on them. A local oysterman disputed that claim, she said. He said that he and a few other oystermen had been taking shifts watching the agents' every move night and day. The evening of the ATF raid they had been working on improving their oyster shucking speed in preparation for the upcoming annual team Shuck Off when they received a call that the agents were gathering outside their motel. The member of team Shuck and Awe who followed the agents to Clara's property said that no one fired on the agents. He said the shots were probably from someone poaching deer on Clara's property. Spooked, the agents stormed the farmhouse and tossed in a flash grenade which set the ancient structure on fire. Flaming debris swept into the air by the inferno fell on the roof of the main house setting it on fire as well. The main house was over a hundred years old and framed with highly resinous heart pine timbers, what the locals call "lighter," was also quickly consumed in flames. The fire department declared the fire too dangerous to contain and issued evacuation orders for residences within a 1-mile radius. Apparently, Clara's husband was a paranoid survivalist who believed that the collapse of civilized society was imminent, and the fire department had issued him a permit to locate an industrial-sized propane gas storage tank close to the house to fuel his own power generation system. That explained the massive explosion. I headed into Apalachicola and left a message for Goose that I wanted to talk.

A few days later Goose dropped by The Essex. The only explanation he could give me for the raid was that they had received "actionable intelligence." I blamed him for what happened, and I believed he blamed himself for how badly it all went down. His supervisors at ATF felt the same way. They were under a lot of scrutiny after receiving national media attention and the resulting public outcry, comparing what happened under his supervision to the Branch

Davidian debacle in Waco, Texas. Goose was put on paid leave until a full review of the facts and circumstances of the failed raid was completed. He explained to me that in the chaos that followed when the fires broke out, no one knew with any confidence if Clara was in her home or even if she had been there in the first place.

He said that shortly after the explosion an employee at Apalachicola's general aviation facility reported he had seen Clara's plane take off. No flight plan was filed, and he didn't see who was piloting the plane. The ATF quickly posted an alert, and shortly thereafter it was picked up on coastal surveillance radar. Attempts to make radio contact were unsuccessful as the plane headed out over the Gulf of Mexico. Somewhere over the waters of the Sigsbee Abyssal Plain, it disappeared from radar. A Coast Guard helicopter sent to the site didn't find debris consistent with an aircraft crash. Estimated to be between 12,000 and 14,000 feet deep, the Gulf was simply too deep at that location, to attempt locating plane wreckage. It was assumed that, if the plane did crash, whoever was piloting it had gone down with it. I asked Goose which plane Clara had been flying. He seemed surprised by the question and stated that to his knowledge the only plane she owned was the Beechcraft. He asked if I was aware of another plane. I told him the story of her visit upriver in the small amphibious plane. We surmised that it belonged to a friend, or she was considering buying it. Regardless, Goose seemed certain that there was no record of ownership for a plane other than the Beechcraft. I left it at that.

No human remains were found in the ashes of Clara's home or the Japanese farmhouse and although the investigation into the incident was ongoing, it was widely assumed that Clara was the pilot of the Beechcraft. Because of the intense heat generated by the resin-rich fat lighter framing in the main house, little remained of it and its furnishings except for a large fireproof safety box. Goose told me that no documents of any consequence to the investigation were found in the safe as he handed me a package that Clara obviously had intended for me to have. On a note attached to an old leather valise, she had written my name along with the description of the contents; "Maw-maw's stories." It contained several audio cassettes along with a dozen or so pocket-sized spiral bound notebooks.

I let Gamp know that I needed to be alone. Concerned about my state of mind, she tried to get me to reconsider. Failing that, she insisted on helping me with some shopping, and together we loaded a couple of weeks' worth of groceries and booze onto The Essex. I promised her I wouldn't do anything stupid. She said she would respect my privacy but for only so long before checking in on me. I thanked her for understanding, we hugged, she gave me a peck on the cheek, and I shoved off. She was still standing on the dock when I lost sight of her. That she cared about my well-being touched me.

CHAPTER 15

I honestly don't recall how much time had passed. Maybe it was a few days. Maybe it was a week. Maybe I was still hanging on to the possibility that Clara was still alive, or I was simply in denial. All I remember is that when I began reading her notes and listening to her grandmother's stories I sobered up. I learned that her beloved Maw-maw, Adelaide (Addie) Parkman Blackwell, was her maternal grandmother. The accounts of her life included tales of hardship and suffering as well as wealth and privilege. I was humbled by them. Addie was not only bound and determined to survive no matter what life threw at her, but she was also equally determined to thrive.

Addie was born in Boston on September 1, 1893 to Maria and Thomas Parkman. Thomas was the heir of a railroad fortune. Addie was the third of five children, but her sisters died in infancy and her brothers in their early twenties. Although medical science was advancing rapidly in the last half of the 19th century, infant mortality rates were high; even if you survived childhood, the average life expectancy was just over 40 years. She was the only child to live past the age of twenty-five. At the age of six, she was sent to a Catholic boarding school. Her father was killed two years later when the train he was riding on crossed a bridge that collapsed. She returned home to live with her mother; her grandmother, whose husband died in the Civil War; and her great-grandmother whose husband died of "consumption." It was her grandmother who oversaw her education and taught her French and the piano. Until her mother (Old Maw-Maw) remarried, when Addie was sixteen, she had grown up surrounded by smart, courageous, single women.

At the age of twenty, Addie married Aaron Aucoin, twenty-five, and the only son of a wealthy cotton-growing family from Louisiana. She and Aaron met and fell in love on Martha's Vineyard where his family owned a summer home. By all accounts he adored Addie and admired her independence and intelligence; she enjoyed unheard of freedoms for a woman. After their marriage, they lived in New Orleans where she had three girls—Emma, Agnes, and Grace—in three years and in that order. On occasion, she traveled with her husband to Apalachicola to look after his father's investments in the region's burgeoning timber and turpentine industry. Aaron's father was shot to death outside a popular New Orleans restaurant when he was caught in the crossfire of a shootout between the rival Matranga and Provenzanos Mafia crime families.

Aaron inherited the business but not his father's business acumen. Soon, he was no longer able to afford the expense of New Orleans high society. Renting out their Garden District home, they moved to the old family plantation in a small Louisiana parish. With Addie's help, Aaron managed to stabilize the business, but a few years later he contracted equine infectious anemia and died. Under Addie's able management the plantation prospered. Tragedy struck again during the great influenza pandemic of 1918 when her two older daughters contracted the disease while accompanying Addie on a business trip in New Orleans. At the time, there were no effective drugs or vaccines to treat this killer flu strain or prevent its spread. In New Orleans alone, a city of 370,000 in 1918, over 55,000 people were infected, and thousands died, including her daughters.

In 1922 she sold the plantation for a large sum. Since there was a surge in corporate sawmill expansion going on in the Apalachicola River basin, she held on to a few thousand acres of timberland. The property included a two-story Greek Revival home on a bluff overlooking the Apalachicola River that Aaron's father had built for his mulatto mistress. The home was one of the grandest houses on the Apalachicola at the time. This would be the house and timberlands that Clara eventually inherited along with the original family home in New Orleans. Addie and her surviving daughter, Grace, returned to Boston and moved into a suite at the iconic Omni Parker House hotcl. Addic placed her in the same Catholic boarding school she had attended as a girl and proceeded to lose herself in the cultural explosion that was the Roaring Twenties.

In her writing, Clara inserted notes that were more sociological in nature that led me to think that she had been considering authoring a book about her grandmother's life and times. Regarding the Roaring Twenties she wrote: "World War I had a tremendous influence on my grandmother's generation. The 'Great War' had forced them to grow up quickly. Beginning in 1914 and ending in 1918, millions of soldiers had been affected by the horrors of battle. After seeing pointless death on such a huge scale, many lost their faith in traditional values. Some became aimless, reckless, and focused on material wealth, unable to believe in abstract ideals. Their heroic contributions were too often not acknowledged; this led to deep disillusionment. Skepticism about the role of government became more prevalent among younger people and eventually extended to all forms of authority. The 'Lost Generation' started exploring its own set of values, ones that defied the established order. Rebellious, they came up with more liberal social mores that fueled their self-indulgent spree. However, the party came to a screeching halt when the stock market crashed on Tuesday, October, 29 1929. Black Tuesday, is remembered as the beginning of the Great Depression. Drawn into the whirlpool of panic selling that beset the New York Stock Exchange, the Boston Stock Exchange, lost over 25 percent of its value in two days of frenzied trading. The stock market continued its slide, and by its lowest point in July of 1932, the market had lost nearly 90 percent of its value."

In one of her taped sessions with Clara, Addie recalled Black Tuesday saying, "Many of my friends felt that they could multiply their fortunes by investing in the stock market. Some invested everything they had and, on top of that, bought even more stock on credit. Although the stock market had the reputation of being risky, they seemed to forget that. Everyone was feeling so optimistic. You know, inventions such as the airplane and radio made anything seem possible back then. And the more people invested, of course the higher the stocks went up. Stocks were the talk of the town. Wherever you went you would hear people talking about stocks. As newspapers reported stories of ordinary people— like chauffeurs, maids, and teachers— making millions, I guess the stock market started to seem like a sure thing. I was tempted a time or two to give it a shot, but I stuck with my preference to invest my money in things I could see, taste, and touch. Glad I didn't get caught up in all that greed. That's all it was. Greed. People I knew lost everything they had. Ruined their lives. A few killed themselves over it. How sad is that?"

"Things started to get bad in Boston. People were tossed out of their homes and as the evictions increased, families moved in together in crowed apartments to avoid living on the streets. Some men who had been quite well off became tramps drifting from neighborhood to neighborhood looking for any work or handout they could find.

The lucky ones, if you can call them that, had access to vacant lots where they planted vegetables to keep from going hungry. Those worse off starved, even eating garbage to try and stay alive. That kind of malnourishment brought on a lot of sickness. That's when Grace and I decided to move to this house in Apalachicola I'm sitting in talking to you right now. That was in1932. Your mother had just turned sixteen, and she raised such a fuss you could have sworn I was trying to kill her. She got over it, though, the second she saw that beautiful Kostopoulos boy one day at the sponge exchange. Alexios? Grace called him Alex. Took after his daddy, Kal, who owned the exchange. Oh my word, what a sexy looking man Kal was! Greek immigrants. They did well until the red tide hurt the sponges. That was about 1939, I think. Alex was the first of many suitors your mother had. Between you and me I wouldn't say Grace was the most beautiful girl in town at the time, but she had something the guys couldn't resist, my sweet baby. She was one of those girls who got more beautiful as she matured. You know what I mean, dear? Your poor dad, god rest his soul, didn't stand a chance when she had him in her sights."

On a separate tape Addie share's her memories of Clara's father, Sam Butterfield. "The way it was told to me, Sam ran away from home at the age of 10 to work as a cabin boy on a sternwheeler. It was the P.W. Morse, one of the fancier ones, and it ran from Columbus, Georgia to Apalachicola. Smart as a whip and quite determined, your dad worked his way into the engine room where he eventually learned enough to earn an engineer's license. Then he wormed his way into the pilothouse every chance he could get so he could learn the pilot's trade. When he was just 16 years old the captains he had been working with went on strike. He remembers sitting on the dock in Columbus wondering what to do with himself when Mr. Charlie Brunson, the president of the navigation company that owned the Morse, drove up in a chauffeured limousine. When Sam told the story to me, he described Mr. Brunson as being so fat and angry he thought he might explode. Speaking to Sam from a distance, seemingly afraid to get some dirt on himself or something, he asked if Sam could "carry" the boat to Apalachicola, meaning, could he pilot the boat. Sam said he'd have to talk to the captains about it first. He respected people that way, your dad, it seems even as a boy. They told him this was his big chance as the boats weren't going to be running much longer.

As they say, the rest is history. Sam was one of the last to pilot sternwheelers. Trucks and railroads changed all that. That's when he settled in Apalachicola and starting building shrimp trawlers. Some of them 50, 60 feet. Beautiful boats. The Greeks were building them too in St. Augustine, but Sam's were something else. Couldn't build them fast enough. Your mother was a quiet child, not shy, just private, so I'm not certain when or how she and Sam met. Seemed they were pretty much already in love by the time she first brought him around the house. Sam was older than her by eight years, and, being out on the river and all since he was a boy, he looked a bit weathered. Older looking than his years I guess I'm saying. He had these deep, dark eyes. Sort of mysterious looking in a Humphrey Bogart kind of way. Good looking, though, and a stand-up fellow. They married when Grace turned twenty after courting a respectable amount of time. Both were set on getting married out in the Gulf on the deck of one of Sam's boats. Small wedding too. No bridesmaids or groomsmen. Just me, them, and the boat's captain. Captain married them. That was your mother; she marched to the beat of her own drum. They set up house on the island, and you came along a couple years later. Those three years before we got pulled into the war were the happiest days of your mother's life.

After Pearl Harbor Sam signed up. The draft started taking them from 18 to 35 but your dad, he was very patriotic. He wanted to get out there and kill some Germans. Since his whole life up 'til then had been all about boats, it was no surprise to anyone that he ended up as an officer commanding a sub chaser. They were in the North Sea when they took a hit and sank. It was October. No one could have survived in that ice-cold water. You and your mother moved in with me. Life can be so cold and cruel. It was like I was reliving the time when I was a child after my father died and my mother and I moved in with my grandmother, except it was all the other way around. You were just four years old. Probably too young to remember much about what went on back then, but your mother was never the same. What's that? You want to what? Oh, I'm so sorry dear. Yes, let's not . . ."

That's how that story ended. I listened to the others, expecting that Clara would want to hear more from Addie about her father, but he didn't come up again. Mysteriously, in later recordings the only times Addie spoke of Clara's mother were stilted references to visiting her in the "mental home." Addie died on March 17,1984 and was buried in the Magnolia Cemetery in Apalachicola. Clara's mother, Grace, could, as of this writing, still be alive. She would be 96 years old. Clara never mentioned her to me, and I wondered if she was still living. I made a note to ask Gamp what she knew.

Listening to Addie's stories about the great challenges and suffering that Clara's family endured, helped me look at my own unhappiness in a more universal light and somehow that made it easier to bear. The suffering in these stories also turned my attention back to Yoku and what I learned from her about how Buddhists placed suffering into three different types: The "suffering of suffering;" meaning the pain of birth, old age, sickness, and death. The "suffering of change." Getting what you want but cannot hold onto it. Meaning, no matter how successful we are or how much wealth we acquire, we will eventually lose it all; and "all-pervasive suffering," a type of suffering most people generally do not recognize. She described it as the background of anxiety and insecurity in our lives that affects us deep down and colors even our happiest moments.

Yoku's practice of Buddhism as she explained to me always seemed rational and rooted in psychology rather than the supernatural. It didn't require of her that she believe six impossible things before breakfast. That it had some intellectual respectability made it interesting and appealing to me but not enough to move me away from what is generally called Naturalism.

A Naturalist's view of the world is based on evidence. Naturalists see the natural world as a closed system and that all phenomena can be explained in terms of natural causes and laws. Questions about what exists for a Naturalist are basically scientific questions, rather than philosophical or religious questions. Naturalists don't believe in the supernatural. However, Naturalism didn't offer me much in the way of soothing any kind of psychic suffering. It was Yoku's unspoken assurances of love—hugs, holding hands, cuddling on the couch, an unexpected kiss, even a pat on the back that helped ease my existential pains more than anything else.

A friendly hug, like Gamp and I have shared, feels to me like a mix of the natural and the artful. It's natural because bodily contact is that first, endorphin releasing language we learn as babies. Artful, because it's an action that must be synchronized with someone else. In the absence of touch, we become hungry for it. The tender touch of others is now known to boost the immune system, lower blood pressure, decrease the level of stress hormones and trigger the release of the same kind of opiates as painkilling drugs.

CHAPTER 16

Over the decades that I had been involved in various environmental causes at local, national, and international levels, the most common words I heard spoken time and time again among environmentalists were, "We're fucked." Yet, hoping against hope, these dedicated, law-abiding people desperately fought to defend the natural world with whatever legal tools they had at hand; hoping that it will be okay if this or that piece of legislation got passed, or this or that legislation got defeated, or a Democrat got in the White House, or technology would save the day. But their best efforts to work within the system have been insufficient. Environmentalists continue to lose badly on every front, and they are fearful that things are rapidly getting worse. The day I gave up on hope is also the day when I became a threat to the system that destroys the world that I love.

Unless you have the destructive power of modern military weaponry at your command, it is practically impossible to eliminate a major dam in one catastrophic blow. However, with a few hundred thousand dollars, lots of patience, and a little ingenuity, compromising the structural integrity of a dam like Buford Dam until it fails would be possible. Not unlike humans, dams have their own age-related vulnerabilities and Buford Dam, being over fifty years old, is not an exception.

On March 1, 1950, seven men each turned over a spade of dirt in what was a symbolic start of the construction of a dam in northern Gwinnet County, Georgia. Breaking ground originally referred to the first step in preparing soil for cultivation. Breaking ground later came to mean the initiation of a construction project. These men were breaking ground on the Buford Dam project. They were also breaking new ground, meaning this dam would advance dam design beyond previous technological achievements. Like dams constructed in the early 1900s the powerhouse would still need to be tied to rock or concrete walls, but unlike earlier dams Buford was engineered to plug the Chattahoochee River with a series of "saddleback" dams created from gravel and dirt. These types of dams are not surprisingly called "earthen" dams.

The first half of the 20th century saw a boom in dam building. Presently there are about 80,000 dams in the United States, 85 percent of them earthen. In a 2006 report on the nation's infrastructure the American Society of Civil Engineers gave America's dams a grade of "D," warning that there are "just too many aging dams and too few safety inspectors." At the time, the average age of dams in the United States was 51. Numerous dams had failed due to internal erosion. In the 70s, five major dam failures took hundreds of lives and caused almost $1.5 billion in damage: three of those failures were attributed to internal erosion.

Internal erosion is one of the most common causes of earthen dam failures. It's the removal of soil particles from the embankment, foundation or abutments of a dam by water seeping through the dam. If the seepage that discharges at the downstream side of the dam carries particles of soil, an elongated cavity or "pipe" may be eroded backward toward the reservoir through the embankment, foundation or an abutment. When a backward-eroding pipe reaches the reservoir, a catastrophic breaching of the dam will almost certainly occur. Internal erosion is exceptionally dangerous because it can occur with little or no external evidence that it is occurring. By the time internal erosion becomes evident, an earthen dam could possibly breach within hours.

Internal erosion on an earthen dam can't be completely prevented but damage caused by internal erosion can be limited by frequent, thorough inspections and prompt maintenance. This assumes that the inspector involved in inspecting the dam understands the causes of internal erosion and can read the subtle signs that it is occurring. There is worry that some owners, especially private ones, may not have the desire or financial ability to maintain their dams properly. Adding to the concern is the fact that states regulate about 95 percent of thc country's dams, and many states have underfunded dam safety programs. Each state dam inspector oversees, on average, 216 dams. One way I could see to take down Buford Dam might be to compromise a dam inspector.

But blackmailing or bribing a dam inspector to look the other way would let the dam fail at some unpredictable point in the future. That wasn't the answer. The destruction of Buford Dam had to be predictable, allowing enough time for warning tens of thousands of people to get out of harm's way. Years ago, The Corps of Engineers discovered seepage in Saddleback No. 3 when the Lake was above full pool. They elected to keep an eye on the seepage site and not remediate the issue because the Lake is rarely allowed to be above full pool for an extended period. I thought maybe a small explosive device set off in the seepage zone on the reservoir side of the leaking saddleback could enlarge the seepage path enough to allow the pressure of billions of gallons of impounded water to complete the demolition. But Lake Lanier is rarely allowed to rise 1085 feet above sea level. This is known as the flood pool level. Based on the projected impact of weather systems in, or approaching, the area, water releases to lower the reservoir begin well before the Lake reaches flood pool levels.

However, if the controls in the powerhouse that regulate discharges from Lake Lanier could be disabled when the Lake is rising and approaching flood pool, this would put immense pressure on the saddlebacks. The Buford Dam powerhouse itself is surrounded by barbed-wire fencing and surveillance cameras. None of these precautions existed before Sept. 11, 2001. After those terrorist attacks, a generous influx of federal Homeland Security money was distributed to make sure that no one could compromise the dam. Before the "internet of things," restricting physical access was all the security needed to protect power-generating facilities. Just keep the bad guys from literally getting their hands on your facility was the strategy. In 2009 the interlinking of the physical world and cyberspace was well underway. The ability to connect, communicate with, and remotely manage an incalculable number of networked, automated devices wirelessly or via the Internet was becoming pervasive, from the factory floor to the ocean floor, from living rooms to the command centers of hydroelectric dams.

Buford Dam in fact no longer had a command center on site. The powerhouse workers there were merely care takers who kept the dam healthy but had no say in how much water goes through it. The plant was controlled by a microwave signal received from the command center of Carters Dam some 70 miles away. The amount of water to be released each day was decided by officials at the Corps of Engineers' district office in Mobile, Alabama. Intercepting the microwave signal and hacking the command center controls was another possibility to be seriously explored.

The challenges were significant: learn how to identify the seepage site on Saddleback No. 3, position an explosive charge in the reservoir side of the seep without being caught, and hack the microwave signal controlling releases from Lake Lanier at Buford Dam. Then, wait for that moment when the Lake was rising and projected to reach flood pool levels. Driven by every unanswered wrong that I had experienced in my life and obsessed with delivering retribution not just for myself but also for the Apalachicola, the Chattahoochee, and the Flint, I was undaunted. It had all come down to choosing sides in a war between civilization and the rivers, and I chose the rivers.

CHAPTER 17

Just as suddenly and shockingly Bernie Madoff emptied my pockets, they were full again. As my accountant explained it, Madoff originally transferred my money into a Spanish bank account. The bank, in turn invested my money through Bernie's brokerage firm. This little trick apparently was intended to reduce his "exposure," or something to that effect, in the event everything went to hell, as it eventually did. When the trustee in charge of liquidating Bernie's brokerage firm and recovering funds from the scandal uncovered the fraud, he forced the bank to settle for the entire amount. Of the people that did get money back, only a few were "made whole." Tens of thousands of investors had been ripped off by Madoff and only about 1,300 had their full investments recovered. That I was one of the fortunate few may have had something to do with the Spanish bank president being a fan of my writing. My accountant was told by the trustee that the president of the bank had read all my books and felt terrible that I got screwed and to please extend to me his personal apology.

It was a great relief to be financially sound again and I felt like spending some money. It was going to take considerable amounts of cash and patience to get to where the fate of the Buford Dam, and possibly every dam in the Apalachicola-Flint-Chattahoochee river basin, lay in my hands. I was flush with both.

It was getting on two weeks since I had gone into Apalach, and I was running low on supplies. Gamp had also become concerned that I had been spending too much time alone and called a few times to invite me to join her for this or that event. I missed her company, but I was not ready for any kind of social activity. Reluctantly, I headed down river after sunset to avoid seeing the burned out remains of Clara's home and the old farmhouse.

Arriving near midnight at my mooring below the Last Cast, I decided to go on up and see if Gamp was still open. I walked into a scene strongly reminiscent of my first visit to the "Cast." At the bar, a dozen or so oystermen swiveled their heads in unison towards me. Gamp, like the first time, was behind the bar and on the bar top directly in front of her was a box or large book, just as before. This time the oystermen kept their seats and Gamp left the box on the bar as she came to me, gave me a big hug, explained that her book club had just finished discussing their latest read, and invited me to share some powdered donuts and coffee with them. Powdered donuts! That explained the white dust on the bar top I suspected was cocaine on my first visit. Book club? That was a little hard to believe. My reception by the oystermen was more welcoming this time and there were smiles and handshakes as Gamp introduced me to each of them.

Still curious about the book club thing, I asked what they were reading. Gamp explained that they were more of a reading club than a book club and that every month during the school year, they, and over 60 other volunteers, read the Book-of-the-Month to more than 4,000 elementary students throughout the county. Copies of the book were also placed in each of the classrooms and library of each school.

"We meet here once a month and talk about the book that we'll be reading to the students. Want to join? This month's book is about marine life. The donuts and coffee are on me." I told her that I would give it some thought. "We can talk more later," she said. I was embarrassed at how seriously wrong I read this situation the first time.

When I started writing professionally, I had the standard collection of reference books: books that focused on the mechanics of writing: style, editing, grammar; books that focused on structure; books about navigating the unique inner life of a writer; an unabridged dictionary, a thesaurus, a book of quotations. With the advent of the internet and social media, resources for writers exploded and one of my favorites became the Urban Dictionary. It's an online dictionary that anyone can make a submission to. At first the Urban Dictionary was intended as a dictionary of slang, of cultural words or phrases that were not typically found in standard dictionaries. It eventually became a repository for definitions of any word. The same words may even be given multiple definitions. It soon devolved into a platform for societies' cynics and sickos to express themselves, but I always found it fascinating as a social enterprise. It could frequently be disturbing but on occasion refreshingly insightful.

There are multiple definitions of Urban Dictionary on Urban Dictionary. One of my favorites was, "An outlet for word addicts, who can be grouped into six main characters: the rarely creative, the hypocritically cynical, the politically irreverent, the sexually depraved, the religiously racist, and the sarcastically narcissistic. On a lighter note, the Urban Dictionary motivates us not to take life seriously— "let's laugh at our idiocies and idiosyncrasies, not to say, our frailties and fatalities."

Upon returning to The Essex after coffee and donuts, I got onto the Urban Dictionary site and looked up "jaded." This is what came up: "The end result of having a steady flow of negative experiences, disappointment, and unfulfillment fed into a person where they get to the point where their anger circuits just sort of burn out and they accept disillusionment." "Cynical, disbelief in the sincerity of human motives, believe that the worst will happen, pessimistic." And lastly, "A state of disillusionment and sadness. You see through everything and have no illusions about what is true. So many negative things have happened that it becomes difficult to stay positive about what once gave you hope and joy. Sometimes you might think there's hope, but then more negative things happen in the aspect you are jaded in, and you become more jaded. This can be felt in many different aspects: love, friendship, politics, trust, music, objects, etc." Sometimes the Urban Dictionary hits closer to where you live than Webster does. I thought to myself that reading to children might be a soul redeeming thing to do and made a mental note before turning in for the night to talk to Gamp about getting involved in the program the next time I went in for a drink.

"So, do you think reading to kids makes it okay for you to drown their little asses! Have you lost your fucking mind? Seriously, Eirik, what has happened to you? Even if nobody dies, and there ain't no way in hell you're going to pull that off SIR, what you're talking about will screw up the lives of thousands of people! WHAT IS WRONG WITH YOU?"

Gamp was furious and insisted I leave the Last Cast immediately before she said something that she would regret. After talking to her about the reading program, and having one too many tequilas, I'd impulsively decided to divulge my dam-busting scheme. Looking back, I know why I disclosed my plan to Gamp—it was an insane idea concocted in a bitter, angry moment of spitefulness and I knew she wouldn't hesitate to tell me so.

It was weeks later, after agonizing over whether I should stay in Apalachicola or not, that I decided it would be best for me to move to the Keys. Gamp didn't understand. She tried to persuade me to stay and apologized for being so harsh in her judgement of me. I told her that I was grateful for her calling me out on what was undoubtedly psychopath-class thinking. I explained that in the aftermath of what happened with Goose and Clara, I needed to get away. I left open the possibility that I would return. She wanted to know if I'd be taking The Essex. I said no but that I would like to keep her moored at The Last Cast until I decided whether to keep or sell her if she was okay with that. She said that was fine and we agreed that I would continue to pay the same dockage fee to her that I'd been paying all along. I told her I'd kick in an extra month's fee once I got settled, if she would pack up the small library I kept on The Essex and have it shipped to me. She said not to worry about paying her. I also invited her to take The Essex out periodically if she cared to. She said that she just might take me up on that offer. We held on to each other in the Last Cast parking lot until it got awkward. I said goodbye. She said she was going to miss me and to stay in touch. I said I was going to miss her too and got into my rental car and drove away.

CHAPTER 18

As an activist I was constantly trying to build support for the issues I thought needed to be addressed. There was nothing more infuriating to me than watching people who I wanted to believe were "good" people just standing there doing nothing while something awful was happening. Witnessing time and time again apathy in the face of injustice eventually eroded my confidence in the goodness of mankind. Frustration and disillusionment led to anger and despair. It was apparent to me that my ill begotten plan to monkey wrench Buford Dam was born out of rage and an overwhelming sense of hopelessness.

At especially low points soon after Yoku's death, when I was drinking heavily, I attended a few AA meetings. It was in those meetings that I learned what is known as the Serenity Prayer; the common name for a prayer written by the American theologian Reinhold Niebuh. AA used the best-known form.

God, grant me the serenity to accept the things I
cannot change,

Courage to change the things I can,
And wisdom to know the difference.

Niebuh wrote the prayer for a sermon in the early 30s. There were precursors that presented similar sentiments. Friedrich Schiller advocated in 1801: "Blessed is he, who has learned to bear what he cannot change, and to give up with dignity, what he cannot save." Six hundred years preceding Schiller was this by the 11th century Jewish philosopher, Solomon Gabirol. He wrote: "At the head of all understanding – is realizing what is and what cannot be, and the consoling of what is not in our power to change."

As a writer I generally avoid platitudes; they tend to oversimplify what are complicated subjects. Yoku's death was not complicated, and the prayer did lead me to eventually accept something I obviously could not change. However, I knew that I couldn't "give up with dignity" that which I still hoped could be saved. I also knew that I needed to look at the challenge of affecting change differently before I ended up destroying myself or others. After decades of relentless effort, I had become deeply entrenched in my thinking about how to change the world. Failing that, I was uncertain to how I was going to go about affecting change within myself.

Of one thing I *was* certain; I was ready to put down my "pen." Writing is intense work. As Annie Dillard characterizes it in "*The Writing Life*," a piece of writing is a "line of words" that a writer follows to its natural, even unexpected, end. Then, there is the cutting away of words, scenes, chapters, and characters that get in the way of that line being both followed and interpreted clearly by a reader. She suggests that the line is connected to the writer's heart, and as such will, if the line is followed truthfully, connect to the heart of the reader. But truth and heart aside, just getting words to the page requires focus, diligence, courage, and a surplus of optimism. Even when I was highly motivated to follow that line of words, it was always damn hard work. My articles, essays, and novels had been read by millions and I enjoyed a level of success that eludes most authors. With much of my hard-earned fortune restored, I was ready to retire from the writing life.

In the '80s, the Italian journalist and author Tiziano Terzani, after many years of reporting across Asia, retreated to a cabin in Ibaraki Prefecture, Japan. Alone for a month, he passed the time with books, observing nature, "listening to the winds in the trees, watching butterflies, enjoying silence." He remarked that for the first time in a long while he felt free from the incessant anxieties of daily life and, "At last I had time to have time."

Humans have long stigmatized solitude. It has been considered something to avoid, a punishment, a realm of loners. I didn't find Tiziano's embrace of seclusion unusual. In times of personal turbulence throughout my life, I have spent a few hours or days in solitude to sort things out. After all I had been through, I decided that I would take all the time I needed to put myself back together and would retreat to an island in the Florida Keys, Palaita, for a year, maybe longer.

Islands are often imagined as utopias. In humankind's constant struggle to conquer and possess the world at large, these micro continents offer the illusion of possession, control, freedom from vice, autonomy, and self-determination—places where one can follow his heart, live by her own rules.

As islands go, my island is small, an islet. It's in a cove offshore from a nature preserve. There are no homes along the shoreline of the cove, ensuring a sense of solitude although Palaita is only a 15-minute boat ride from Marathon Key. Marathon is a fully functioning, "family-friendly" community with grocery stores, dive shops, a hospital, museums, airport, and numerous restaurants along with tourist attractions. There are no cars on Palaita. Consequently, there are no streets, streetlights, stoplights, stop signs, gas stations, stores, restaurants, neighborhoods, or neighbors. Palaita is tucked away, and I hear no mechanical sounds other than the occasional airplane flying overhead or fishing boat cruising by. Unless by my invitation, there is no one on Palaita other than myself.

Other than a dock extending out beyond a fossilized reef to deeper waters, the single structure there is a modest-sized, two-bedroom, one-bath West Indies style cottage. It has numerous tall windows to admit light and cool breezes, a large wraparound porch, a steeply pitched metal roof, and high vaulted ceilings on the interior.

The house is equipped with the devices and appliances that can enable one to live off the grid: a propane-fueled refrigerator, a solar electric power system, a gasoline-powered generator to back up the solar system, a cistern to store rainwater for drinking and bathing, solar hot water, a low-water toilet, and an eco-friendly septic system. There is no air conditioning, no TV, no wi-fi, and marginal cell phone service. It does have a battery-powered marine VHF radio for checking on the weather and for possible emergencies.

The island's amenities most important to me were lush tropical foliage, sandy canopied pathways, a secluded beach, generous offerings of peace and quiet, an unobstructed view of the horizon, and a solitary 50-foot Sabal Palm that towered above all else on the island. It's likely that there were once more Sabal Palms on Palaita, but a disease called Lethal Bronzing that's spread by a rice-sized, plant-hopping insect has gone from a small infestation on Florida's Gulf Coast to a nearly statewide problem in just over a decade. Tens of thousands of palm trees have died from the bacterial disease. Trees not yet infected can be protected with injections of oxytetracycline hydrochloride given every three to four months for at least two years. Not knowing if Palaita's last Sabal Palm had been treated and, if so, for how long, I started giving it injections with the assumption that it hadn't. It looked healthy, but there was a possibility it had already been infected and symptoms of the disease had just not yet appeared. I had failed the planet, but I wasn't going to allow Sabal Palms to become extinct on *my* island.

As a writer, the horizon is familiar to me mostly as a semi-mythical distance that is often used metaphorically. But in fact, it is a knowable "thing." Calculating the distance to the farthest point the eye can see before the Earth curves out of view depends simply on the height of the observer, knowing the radius of the Earth, and applying the genius of Pythagoras's theorem.

Imagine me on my beach. I am standing looking out over the ocean to the horizon. My eyes are five feet and six inches above sea level. The radius of the Earth is 3,959 miles. Applying the theorem, I can calculate that the horizon, from my individual point of view, is 3 miles away.

Other than this line where the earth appears to meet the sky, it's common to see horizon used to illustrate a conceptual or perceptual experience such as, he left home to broaden his horizons, or her discovery opened new horizons in the field of cancer. In this excerpt from her poem, "On the Pulse of Morning," Maya Angelou uses horizon metaphorically as a source of inspiration and hope.

"Lift up your eyes upon
The day breaking for you.

Give birth again
To the dream.

Women, children, men,
Take it into the palms of your hands.

Mold it into the shape of your most
Private need.
Sculpt it into
The image of your most public self.

Lift up your hearts.

Each new hour holds new chances
For new beginnings.

Do not be wedded forever
To fear, yoked eternally
To brutishness.

The horizon leans forward,
Offering you space to place new steps of
change."

I was still mourning the death of old dreams after leaving Apalachicola and hadn't felt inspired to conjure up new ones. Each day I woke at dawn and walked out to the beach with a cup of tea wearing nothing but my mortality and looked out to the eastern horizon to watch the morning break. *My* horizon had yet to offer me anything. Out of that act did come a bit of comfort in knowing that it was a measurable three miles away and therefore as immutable as the sunrise. After trying to affect change in the world for most of my adult life and experiencing years of emotional upheaval, the sunrise and this simple calculable constant were reassuring.

CHAPTER 19

My mother was a lover and caretaker of all creatures big and small and made our home a haven for a wide assortment of wild and domestic animals: baby possums, a crow, an egret, squirrels, a raccoon, cats, dogs, parakeets, rabbits, hamsters, turtles, and snakes. Rarely was a stray or wounded animal not taken in. She treated amphibians, fish, mammals, and reptiles with the same care and respect usually reserved for people, and they responded to her with obvious affection.

I inherited her compassion for what she called the "little people." However, I recall that she was not all that big-hearted when it came to invertebrates, especially arachnids. I wouldn't say she was arachnophobic, but those poor spider guys didn't stand a chance if they made it into her home. I don't know exactly when I began to put them in the same category as all other animals and accept them as pets and even sometimes as roommates.

Kuku lived behind the headboard of my island home bed. It was her home before I arrived. I figured she had a squatter's rights. Kuku is commonly known as a southern house spider or southern crevice spider. Her proper name is *Kukulcania hibernalis*. I had no idea how old she was, but Kukulcanias can live as long as eight years. There was a good possibility she would outlive me.

Most people might be distressed about sharing space with a spider, but I have come to admire Kuku. Unaware of anything beyond her wooly web tucked behind my bed's headboard, she goes about her life. She eats the odd bumbling insect that gets snared in her web, patches up whatever damage her unfortunate prey may have inflicted in its struggle to break away, and then goes back to trusting that a universe functioning in the same perfect order it has for eons will deliver her next meal. I can depend on her day in and day out to just be herself. Her world spins exactly as it must, and she's not distracted or disheartened by bad news or a broken web. She's also not restricted by any laws imposed upon her by her species that would cause her to repress an innate irrepressible urge to devour her tiny husband because she is starving.

Cannibalism strikes the human conscience like few other taboo acts, eliciting a mix of dread, disdain and plain old nausea. However, human beings also have a fierce instinct to survive. Any shopper walking down the aisles of a modern grocery is overwhelmed with choices when it comes to food options. The number of products carried by the average supermarket is measured in the tens of thousands, and it's hard to imagine that there is substantial evidence throughout history that rather than starve, humans eating other humans was not an uncommon practice. After the whaleship "Essex" was sunk by a vengeful sperm whale, its crew was left on the high seas for 90 days, causing them to resort to cannibalism. I didn't disturb Kuku but occasionally, out of sympathy for her tiny male companion, I dropped into her web a fly that I had managed to stun with a lucky swipe of my hand.

Kuku was the first of a menagerie of animals on the island that I came to interact with not as pets but as individuals with intrinsic value separate from the worth they came to have to me as companions. I identified five species of snakes on Palaita: corn, rat, ringneck, black racer, and the Brahminy Blind Snake. Brahminys are tiny; at first I mistakenly thought they were earthworms. Green anoles, brown anoles, and scrub lizards thrived on the island. They all seemed to enjoy hanging out around the porch and regularly made their way inside the house along with the occasional Mediterranean Gecko. Med Geks are about 3-5 inches long and cream-colored. During mating season, they sing the sweetest little chirping songs.

A single common green iguana I named Iggy calmly strolled around near the shoreline. It sought out the sunniest spots where it would bask for hours. Iggy seemed lonely to me, but I didn't know much about iguanas' social behavior. They do copulate to reproduce, so it is not a stretch to assume that Iggy might like a mate if only for a one-night stand.

As my presence became more common to them, and I guess my behavior more predictable, my cohabitants came out of hiding and set about their daily, or nightly, routines. The only routine behaviors that moved with me to Palaita were related to food and drink. And, as far as drink was concerned, I deliberately left my alcohol habit behind in Apalachicola. Once on the island, I consumed nothing but water, tea, fruit juices, and one beer on Sundays.

Minus all the alcoholic drink calories that were normally part of my diet, my weight started to drop. When drinking, I never had a problem falling asleep, but I also rarely felt fully rested. According to numerous studies, alcohol and a good night's sleep don't mix. Alcohol does allow one to fall asleep more quickly, and sleep deeply, but it disrupts REM (rapid eye movement) sleep. REM is the restorative stage of sleep when we dream. And the more you drink before bed, the more pronounced the effect on REM.

After a few weeks off booze, my morning energy levels were higher. I also noticed when shaving that my skin and eyes looked noticeably "brighter." Alcohol is a diuretic and causes you to pee more frequently. What I didn't know was that it interferes with the mechanism that regulates water levels in our bodies, and you end up eliminating *more* urine than normal each time you pee. The combination of these factors leads to dehydration. Typical symptoms of dehydration include dull skin, "shadows" around the face especially under the eyes and around the nose, and increased appearance of fine lines and surface wrinkles. The man in the mirror was starting to look like a younger version of myself!

By trial and error, I discovered the best spot for cell phone service was at the very end of the dock. It extended out beyond the shoals surrounding the island to deeper water in order to accommodate boat access. While on the phone I would sit with my feet dangling in the water. On one particularly hot and humid day, after an extended conversation with Gamp. (To my surprise, she announced she was coming to Marathon Key and would drop off my books rather than ship them. She also mentioned that someone had inquired about buying The Essex.) I stripped off my shorts and jumped in. To swim nude is to swim free. It feels like something the human body was made for. It was at that moment that I began to enjoy swimming again.

I swam competitively when I was in college and, like many college athletes, after years of highly regimented practice routines, forgot what it was I originally loved about swimming. Michael Phelps, who as a child was diagnosed with A.D.H.D, called the pool his "safe haven" explaining that being in the pool slowed down his mind. Swimming for me had a meditative effect that I think was induced by its rhythmic nature and the hypnotic play of light on the bottom of the pool as the sun moved across the lanes. Being submerged and insulated from the constant stimulation modern life bombards us with, also gave my mind space to be free, to stretch, and to wander about.

Years later I wasn't surprised to learn that cognitive scientists using advanced technologies like functional magnetic resonance imaging (FMRI) and electroencephalography (EEG) have gathered evidence that suggests proximity to water, and even recalling aquatic memories, floods the brain with dopamine, serotonin, and oxytocin, the "happy" enzymes. Concurrently, levels of cortisol—that stress-filled enzyme — plummet. Whether choosing to swim in a pool, river, lake, or ocean, each was for me a happy place.

More than water having a feel-good effect, swimming connected me to something deep and primal within myself, something I have come to believe is embedded in human DNA. The simple act of immersing myself in water awakens what feels like an ancient memory. I don't believe I am imagining this. The human body is composed of trillions of cells. All these cells contain a lot of water. In fact, on average, humans are around 65 per cent water. Blood, which is mostly water, is like our own private ocean, and it harkens back to what life was like for the millennia "we" spent drifting as microscopic, single-celled organisms, consuming nutrients from sea water and then eliminating waste back into sea water. Not only is blood mostly water, but the watery portion of blood, plasma, has a concentration of salt and other ions that is remarkably like sea water. Water is essential for life. In fact, NASA's motto in the hunt for extraterrestrial life is "follow the water." We are *of* water, and we *are* water.

I first learned that we were mostly water as a nerdy teenager in a high school biology class. That led me to think that the old phrase, "ashes to ashes, dust to dust" from the English Burial Service, which was derived from the Biblical text, Genesis 3:19, though poetic, was imprecise. I tweaked it to say: In the sweat of thy face shalt thou eat bread, till thou *leach back into the ocean*; for out of it was thou taken; for *water* thou art, and unto *water* shalt thou return. It is a fact that one month after death the human body, unless preserved, will begin to liquefy. Our bones may turn to dust but our tissues, which are mostly what we are made of, turn to water. Water to water.

Swimming in the wilderness that is the open ocean is a vastly different experience from swimming in the highly controlled confines of a pool. The dynamic nature of waves, currents, and changing weather patterns make the ocean far more challenging. Those factors combined with powerful rip tides that can drag you out to sea; the threat of excruciatingly painful stings from jellyfish like the box jellyfish, lion's mane, and Portuguese man of war; aggressive sharks; or toxic algal blooms make it necessary to be extra vigilant while swimming. I decided it would be wise to use mask, snorkel, and swim fins in order to maximize my visibility, maneuverability, and speed.

As a teenager growing up in Florida, I spent endless hours snorkeling its many reefs and springs. Weightless, I imagined I was an astronaut out of this world, or an alien who had come to discover the unknown. Floating along almost effortlessly and hearing nothing except my breath and my heartbeat, I would drift into another state of consciousness. Colors, sounds, and my own thoughts and feelings became deeper and more intense. My imagination took me on beautiful journeys as I soared through mystical underwater worlds.

One of the best coral reefs to snorkel in Florida was just a few miles away from my little island. It was too far for me to swim but easily reachable by boat. After a few weeks of swimming laps around Palaita, I decided to purchase a small power boat typically used by yacht owners to ferry people and supplies to and from shore. They're called tenders. I nicknamed her *Love Me Tender.* I wasn't an Elvis fan, but Yoku loved the slower, spare ballads Elvis crooned in his early years. I rationalized that buying Love Me was for getting to the mainland in the event of an emergency or, the water taxi service I'd been using to go to and from the island was all booked up. That was partially true. My primary motivation was to get out to Sombrero Reef.

It had been decades since I snorkeled Sombrero, or any reef, and far from shore and with not another soul in sight, I was feeling somewhat apprehensive as I tied up to a mooring buoy. As I entered and gazed upon the azure underworld that lay beneath me, I stopped breathing for a moment. It was not from fear; my breath had been taken away by the sudden beauty of it all. I was filled with awe and wonder. For one sparkling moment I was my teenage self again. Unlike many that are dead or dying, Sombrero is still a relatively healthy coral reef, and I struggled to enjoy its vibrancy before my all too well-informed adult self crushed my exuberance. I had little hope that it would escape the deadly effects of rising water temperatures due to climate change, or oceanic acidification, or urban and agricultural runoff and water pollution, which can harm reefs by stimulating excess algal growth. Pick your poison.

CHAPTER 20

Spur and groove features are a distinctive geomorphic characteristic of Sombrero Reef. They are formed by a series of parallel, linear ridges (spurs) separated by channels (grooves) creating finger-like shapes that extend down the reef slope into deeper water on the seaward facing side of the reef. In a shallow groove the sandy bottom may be only 8 feet down or as much 20 feet or more in the deeper grooves.

Snorkeling above the grooves the overall effect is like soaring over mini canyons. In a healthy reef system like Sombrero, sea life in the seaward zone is diverse and abundant and the canyons are alive with movement and color. There are corals and sponges with eponymous names that evoke shapes and colors like Pillar, Elkhorn, and Brain Coral, Green Finger Sponge, Red Boring Sponge, and Black-Ball Sponge. Peaking and poking about the coral's alcove and cave formations are scores of different fish species with equally eponymous names like Bluehead, Yellowhead Wrasse, Yellowtail Parrotfish, Rainbow Parrotfish, Midnight Parrotfish, and a favorite of mine, Blue Tang. Blue Tang bodies are an intense periwinkle color that sets off their voluptuous "lips" and huge eyes. They navigate with delicate, chiffon-like fins, and Bette Midler comes to mind when I see one. There are over 600 species of aquatic creatures in the waters surrounding the Keys, and many more if you include sea birds, marine plants, and amphibians like sea turtles. Of them all, I find turtles the most fascinating.

Evidence gathered from fossils suggest that the early ancestors of modern sea turtles existed over 150 million years ago. That's far back enough to have seen the rise and demise of the dinosaurs. Although sea turtle sightings are reportedly common on Sombrero Reef, I had yet to see one. It was on my fourth visit that I spotted a Leatherback that appeared to be resting under a ledge in the reef no more than 10 feet below. Only the head and a small portion of the upper part of its shell, the carapace, was visible. When active, sea turtles must swim to the surface to breathe every few minutes. When resting, they can remain underwater for as long as two hours. I enjoy watching them "fly." Slow and clumsy on land, they are as graceful and elegant in the water as any bird in the sky. It would be worth the wait for it to awaken and surface. I had no idea how long this one had been napping and, although tempted, I didn't provoke it to move; doing so can frighten sea turtles into staying underwater longer than they should and consequently damage their lungs. I didn't have to wait long.

As the turtle moved out from under the ledge, it was immediately apparent to me that it was in trouble. What I couldn't see when she was tucked under the ledge was a mass of fishing net wrapped around her neck and restricting movement in one of her flippers. Discarded fishing nets are nearly invisible in the dim light of the ocean, and sea creatures unwittingly swim into them. Because the nets are designed to restrict movement after being caught, they can suffer from starvation, cuts, infection, and suffocation. It was obvious to me from her labored movements that she was exhausted from struggling with the net, part of which was cutting into the flesh around her neck and where the entangled flipper joined her body. I remained still and let her slowly make her way to the surface before I dove under her, grabbed her on each side of her carapace, and swam over to the tender. She offered little resistance. Kicking furiously with my swim fins, I managed to lift her and myself high enough out of the water to slip her into the boat. After getting back onboard and cutting away the netting, I decided that her wounds were severe enough to take her into the Turtle Hospital on Marathon Key.

The Turtle Hospital is unique in that it was the first state-certified veterinary hospital for sea turtles in the world. It was established in 1986, and its main mission is to treat injured turtles and successfully release them back into the wild. In some cases, individuals are so severely wounded they are deemed "non-releasable" by the Florida Fish & Wildlife Conservation Commission and become permanent residents of the hospital or are adopted by other accredited zoos and aquariums.

The hospital has earned a sterling reputation nationally and internationally. Reportedly, American Airlines has flown injured turtles from as far as South America free of charge. In addition to all its rehabilitation work, the dedicated staff and volunteers at The Turtle Hospital offer educational tours of its facilities, including a viewing window of the operating room in which veterinarians perform surgeries and other treatments.

I headed directly to Marathon Key and called into the hospital's "Stranding Hotline" as soon as I had cell service. I was told that a Save-A-Turtle volunteer would meet me at Sombrero Beach. Save-A-Turtle of the Florida Keys is a volunteer non-profit organization dedicated to the preservation and protection of rare and endangered marine turtles.

Curious to see how my rescue, now named Eirika, was doing, a few days later I decided to go ashore, pick up some supplies, check in on her, and grab dinner. As I pulled up to the hospital, I remembered that the building once housed a bar I had had a few shots in—Fannie's Nude Bar. At the time I rationalized that I was doing a little ethnographic study for a novel I was working on. I did gain some insight into the dancers and patrons and their interactions, but the experience left me feeling sad and I didn't return. As I entered the hospital, I mused that if a nude bar can become a place dedicated to a mission as uplifting as rehabilitating sea turtles, there might be hope for a cynical old barfly like me.

I didn't actively seek celebrity, and it was generally at book signings or when I spoke at writing workshops or conferences that I received requests for my autograph. At home in Florida, it was a different story. My Florida fans were not as enthusiastic in their adoration like Buffet's "Parrotheads" but, when my books were peaking, my true-blue fans, although always polite, did light up upon recognizing me.

As I walked toward the receptionist, she picked up her phone and spoke but a few words in hushed tones before hanging up as I reached her desk. She stood up and, with a huge smile on her face, greeted me warmly, "Welcome Mr. Nilsson, we're so delighted . . . it's just so wonderful . . . what a pleasure . . . thank you. . . we're all so," and just stood there for a moment, her face flushed, before extending her hand. Slightly more composed, she managed to get out her name, shake my hand, and inform me that the director was on her way down to meet me. As we stood there Emily began that nervous little dance some of my shy fans used to do as they worked up the courage to ask me for my autograph. I automatically patted my shirt pocket to see if I had a pen—I didn't.

What I wasn't aware of was that with the advent of smart phones, a selfie taken with one's prized subject was more desirable than an autograph. At the time I knew nothing about selfies so I was confused when Emily held her phone out in front of her and jiggled it while giving me an inquiring look. At first, I thought she was offering me her phone but that didn't make any sense. Picking up on my confusion, she finally managed to speak again and asked if she could take a selfie with me. Not wanting to appear uncool I said yes but really didn't know what I was saying yes to. Obviously pleased at my answer, she came out from behind her desk, positioned herself up against my right side and, with her left arm wrapped around my waist, held her phone out as far she could with her free hand, dropped her head on my shoulder and said, "smile." I dutifully smiled as she took several shots and then previewed them before releasing her arm from around my waist. Pleased with the results she asked if I would like to see the pictures. I felt it was probably proper selfie etiquette to say yes, but at that moment the director of the hospital walked into the reception area and whisked me away.

As we toured the facility, I learned that the hospital is a non-profit organization that utilizes all donated funds entirely for the care of the turtles and has rescued more than 1,000 sea turtles since it was established. Turtles that are deemed incapable of surviving in the wild become an important part of the hospital's educational programs by graphically illustrating the perils that humans can bring upon them.

Many of the staff were college students. Some were locals volunteering to support a worthwhile cause, and others were marine veterinary interns getting real-world experience working with endangered and threatened sea turtles. It had been a long time since I had been around people in their late teens or 20s, and I was moved by their optimism and enthusiasm. I was also surprised that they knew who I was and that they seemed genuinely delighted to meet me—at least I assumed they were because many of them wanted to take a selfie with me.

I felt buoyed by all that youthful energy, and as I was leaving, I impulsively invited them out to Palaita, not really believing they would come. At their age, I certainly would not have wanted to waste a precious summer weekend off with some *old* guy.

CHAPTER 21

As soon as the morning sun clears the horizon each day, Iggy crawls out onto an outcropping of coquina on the east side of Palaita and flattens herself against the porous rock. Because she is cold-blooded, her body doesn't generate its own stable internal temperatures like those of warm-blooded birds and mammals. She basks in the morning sun to raise her internal body temperature that also stimulates her metabolism and limbers up her muscles. In the wild this is crucial for hunting and escaping predators. However, she has no natural predators on the island and, having achieved the status that I would typically bestow on a beloved dog, I regularly supplemented her diet with whatever vegetable cuttings or over-ripe fruit I had on hand. She's not as affectionate as a dog, but if I join her and let the sun bake my naked body, she will slowly crawl over to my side and give me a little lick before settling back down.

When I sunbathe nude I feel a sense of commonality with not only humankind but also with animals. Maybe Iggy's lick is her way of showing approval that I have stripped off that thin layer of civilization that sets me apart from her and other animals. When we are lying out there, we are subjecting ourselves to the same spectrum of radiation from the same source that has powered the evolution of life for billions of years. Every living thing is equal under the sun.

Iggy will move into the shade when she gets too hot. If not careful I fall asleep in the heat which is why when I lay out, I try to remember to set an alarm on my mobile phone (something Gamp taught me how to do). It will randomly pick a song from my playlist and play it at low volume. If I don't turn it off the volume increases a notch, getting louder and louder with each repetition until I awaken. One Saturday morning it *was* music that woke me, but it was not emanating from my phone. It seemed to be coming from somewhere out on the water. Standing and looking toward the dock, I was surprised to see that student volunteers from the Turtle Hospital had taken my invitation seriously.

The origins of pontoon boat design go back thousands of years to ancient people's using logs or inflated animal skins attached to a platform. Were it not for the old, smoking outboard motor powering an obviously geriatric pontoon boat, it would have been hard for me to pinpoint what century it hailed from. However, for everything it lacked in technical sophistication, it more than made up for in ornamentation. It reminded me of the truck art common to Southeast Asia, especially Pakistan. Commercial trucks there are painted in bright colors and literally covered in ornate decorations such as mirrors, chains, motifs (birds, flowers, famous personalities, animals, fish), glittery sheets, stickers, battery-operated lights, jangling chains, beadwork, and woodwork. They are also referred to as "jingle trucks" because the drivers often festoon the exteriors with strings of small bells.

I would later learn that one of the students was a second generation Pakistani who art-directed the decoration of "Sally," the interns' abbreviation for Salacia who in Roman mythology was the female divinity of the sea. Worshipped as the goddess of salt water, she presided over the depths of the oceans. Sally may have never presided, but she did float.

When I stood to locate the source of the music, I forgot for a moment that I was nude. As they approached, a tall, dark-skinned guy with jet black hair was already a fair way up the dock with five or six others not far behind. Seeing me, he stopped and turned shouting excitedly, "He's naked! Mr. Nilsson's naked! It's a clothing optional island," and proceeded to remove his clothing where he stood. There was a collective cheer and shortly the rest of the crew was shedding their clothes as they came.

Unlike most Americans, who are generally very prudish about nudity, I feel comfortable in my own skin. Maybe it is because I have traveled extensively and visited places where public nudity is normal, and locals feel just as comfortable without clothes on as they do with them. In Germany nudism is known as Freikoerperkultur (FKK), Free Body Culture. There, you will see men, women, and children baring it all in saunas, swimming pools, parks, and on the beach.

Germany's passion for taking it all off goes back to late-19th-century health drives when nudity was believed to be a route to fitness and sunbathing a possible cure for TB and rheumatism. In 1920 Germany established its first nude beach on the island of Sylt. Ten years later, the Berlin School of Nudism, which was founded to encourage mixed sex open-air exercises, hosted the first international nudity congress. On the other hand, I think Americans too often equate nudity with sex and partly because of our Puritan heritage, have long associated nakedness and the naked body with sin and shame.

Where I feel the least self-conscious being nude is with close friends about my age and in private settings like a sauna, backyard pool, or an isolated beach. Until that moment on Palaita, I had never experienced a clutch of naked kids, all strangers, running toward me with, as a dear British friend of mine delicately references breasts and genitals, their "wobbly bits" flapping around.

So began the first of many weekend visits. Initially they arrived around midday on Saturdays and went straight to sunbathing, drinking beer, snacking, and diving off the dock to cool down. And, of course, documenting it all with their ever-present smart phones. My conversations with them were superficial and usually took place on their way to or from the toilet as they walked past where I parked myself in the shade up on the porch. Later in the afternoon they would join me for one last beverage. A "sundowner," as Bok, short for Bokomoso, from Cape Town, South Africa referred to it. By this point in the day, they were feeling relaxed, open, and inquisitive. I got the distinct impression that they trusted me and valued my opinion which, I must admit, gave my ego a healthy little boost.

However, needing to get back to the mainland before dark, they would head for Sally just as our conversations were getting juicy. Wanting more time, one day I invited them to bring camping gear when they visited next and sleep over. Much to my delight, for the balance of the summer the same six "kids" (they were all in their early twenties) arrived each Saturday around noon and departed on Sunday before sunset. I learned that they were a tight-knit group whose friendships predated their work at the Turtle Hospital. Given how generally happy and carefree they appeared to be, it would have been easy to idealize their lives. On occasion however, their discussions turned serious and their worries and struggles with money, relationships, or health revealed them not as immature kids having a summer fling but earnest young adults just starting out in the world. Remembering some of my own painful twenty-something life lessons, I felt for them.

Other than the natural beauty of their youthfulness, what was attractive to me were their intriguing questions which gave me some insight into how they viewed the world and what was important to them. I ended up getting to know them as an ensemble of six characters, three men and three women, each with distinctly different personalities.

Rin, who seemed to be the de facto leader of the group, was the fourth generation of American-born Japanese immigrants. She was small but athletic, wickedly smart, and the most cynical of the six. She spoke of growing up poor and working hard for everything in her life. She rarely spoke, but when she did everyone listened.

By contrast, Ashley was from a wealthy New England family and apparently had everything handed to her on a silver platter. Although spoiled and naïve, she had highly developed social skills and could probably charm a snake. She was also curious and ambitious. I felt certain she would not squander her privileged upbringing but use it as a springboard to success.

Luna, the daughter of Pakistani immigrants whose legal first name was Najma, was the most laid back. In my day, us politicos would have considered her a flower child. I thought of her as a neo-hippie. Sweet and kind, her self-professed interest in rehabilitating turtles was simply because "I love those turtle guys." I doubted that her future would be in the hard sciences. However, Rin revealed to me that in graduate school Luna had crushed "numerical linear algebra and mixed finite element methods." Algebra nearly crushed me in college. Luna also played multiple instruments, and it's been my experience that accomplished musicians often excel at math. I, of all people, should understand that you should not judge a book by its cover.

My first impression of Brandon was formed by that sculpted-by-the-sun-and-sea countenance of a surfer: golden tan, long smooth muscles, shoulder length sun-bleached hair, comfortable in his own skin. Like myself, he was a Floridian and, like me, had grown up surfing. His love of ocean creatures was born out of an intimate relationship with the sea. He was quiet and unassuming. It was when sharing his concerns for the planet and humanity that he revealed himself to be compassionate, perceptive, and well informed.

Joshua displayed a range of exaggerated stereotypical masculine behaviors young men of my generation, not yet secure in their sexuality, typically exhibited. The longstanding catch-all descriptor for that kind of behavior is "macho" which may or may not, depending on one's world view, have a negative connotation.

It's my experience that underlying a lot of macho behavior is homophobia. As a mild-mannered, fine featured, "pretty" boy who did not enjoy contact sports, or team sports of any kind, I spent most of my time alone reading or with a couple of close friends either surfing or hanging out on the beach. I was often the target of insults and taunts in high school by boys who presumed I was "queer" or, if not a "fag," at the very least a "pussy." Not finding other boys sexually attractive, being targeted in such a way was confusing. Adding to my confusion, there were also boys, and some men, who found *me* sexually attractive as expressed by everything from direct propositions to pinching my ass and outright sexual assault.

It was not until I was a college student that I seriously considered that maybe there was something about myself that other males could see that I could not. That moment was terrifying in two ways. First I could be reading my own sexual feelings completely wrong. I liked girls, especially girls in those days who were stuck with the label of "tomboy," surfer girls being the most attractive and desirable. Second was the terrifying prospect of being a gay man in what I already understood in the 70s was a society deeply threatened by same-sex sexuality.

It was my first confrontation with my own homophobia. As with racism and sexism, I learned from family members, friends, teachers, newspapers, television, magazines, and movies to be homophobic. Homophobia is pervasive in American society and, consequently, most of us are homophobic to some degree or another, regardless of our sexual orientation.

So, I did what I have done my entire life when confronted with a problem, I read. I consumed everything I could get my hands on about human sexuality and distilled all I learned down to a simple conclusion. Homosexuality is not the problem—the real issue is homophobia. I discovered that in many cultures, same-sex eroticism is socially accepted as part of the normal range of human behavior. But at the time in American society, the view that same-sex sexual contact was disgusting, sick, immoral, or sinful was pervasive.

Being short, chubby, and cute, Joshua's macho displays were almost comical, and the rest of the group obviously, I think to his benefit, was not buying his act. It's my opinion that the earlier the distorted stereotypes we learn as children are challenged and contradicted, the better. His friends, who genuinely seemed to care for him and did a surprisingly good job of calling him on his over-the-top, manly-man bit when it was too much for them to take.

I was a boy once. I suffered the relentless pressure, emotional abuse, and sometimes physical abuse directed at me to suck it up and be a "real man." I had no doubt that any early behavior suggesting Joshua would prefer to be a gentler, nurturing, more "feminine" human being had been figuratively, and maybe literally, beaten out of him by those who feared he was on the road to being queer. I felt for him. He was lucky to have such good friends.

"We move in space with minimum waste and maximum joy" is the lyric from an old Sade song that comes to mind when I think about Bok. Watching him walk was to witness a dimension of humanness that felt perfected and free. I've seen great, highly trained and disciplined artists move with that kind of grace, like when Russian ballet star Mikhail Baryshnikov seemed to defy gravity and fly. The effect was complicated and confusing. There were times I felt dazzled while watching him dance.

Curious, I asked Bok if he had been classically trained and learned that he was not a dancer nor a highly trained athlete. He was a walker. Born and raised in a small South African village, he walked six miles to a school in Cape Town each day. His mornings started before sunrise when he would wake to fetch water, let out the family's cows, and help his younger siblings get ready before setting off on his two-hour trek. Walking was his primary mode of transportation and his primary daily activity.

Yoku studied a movement awareness practice called the Feldenkrais Method. The goal of the Method is to "increase your range of motion, improve your flexibility and coordination, and rediscover your innate capacity for graceful, efficient movement." She was a walker and maintained that learning to walk with efficiency, power, and grace can improve other movements and activities. The rationale is that as you improve the quality of your walking you are also improving the relationship between different parts of yourself and your relationship to the ground.

Out of necessity, Bok walked in pursuit of an education. He didn't have to rediscover his innate capacity for graceful efficient movement because he never lost it. He eventually walked his way into a full scholarship and the Department of Oceanography at the University of Cape Town, where he focused his graduate studies on marine mammals. A successful application for a paid, part-time, summer internship at The Dolphin Research Center in

Grassy Key, Florida brought him to the States for the first time. It was while working at the Center that he learned about the Turtle Hospital. After a visit he decided that he would volunteer.

As the summer progressed, my little tribe fell into a routine. Upon arrival, those who slept on the island rather than the boat, would set up their tents at various favorite sites—some on the water's edge, others sheltered under less exposed (and more private, I assumed) spots in the scrubby areas of the island. Late in the day, after all the swimming and sunning, snacking and drinking, and napping was over, they gathered as a group to have sundowners at the base of Palaita's lone Sabal Palm where they set up camp chairs in a semi-circle facing the palm.

They'd been shocked by my stating it was conceivable that that single palm could one day be the last Sabal Palm in Florida, or even the world. I guessed that unless you witness the death of the last member of a species, extinction lives only as a concept or a shadowy threat. The last Sabal Palm on an island apart from a mainland where a disease was decimating the species, apparently made the threat real for them. It wasn't difficult then to imagine that it was therefore possible for other species of plant or animal to be gone forever.

Gathering around the palm was my favorite activity of the weekend when I would join them as they talked about what was on their minds. Their discussions meandered in different directions depending on what had happened at the Turtle Hospital that week, or what they had been reading, or seen on television, or learned from a lecturer hosted by the hospital. However, their questions to me focused primarily on a single subject and revealed to me that they were concerned that climate change was worsening. They also were feeling like their futures were being sacrificed on a capitalistic altar of greed and irresponsibility. They wanted to be assured there was still time to save the planet.

Climate change represents the collapse of complex systems at such an extreme scale that it overrides our emotional capacity, and we experience feelings of grief and anxiety. The concept of eco-anxiety was beginning to enter the mainstream vocabulary. Psychotherapists were finding that the constant specter of environmental decay was having a physiological impact on younger people's lives even though they were not caught in a disaster. A survey of 10,000 people, aged 16 to 25, conducted in 10 countries, published in *The Lancet*, an international scientific medical journal, found "startling rates of pessimism." Forty-five percent of respondents said anxiety about climate change negatively affected their daily life. Three-quarters said they believed "the future is frightening," and 56 percent said, "humanity is doomed." Susan Clayton, a professor of psychology at the University of Wooster, has observed that "The blow to young people's confidence appears to be more profound than with previous threats, such as nuclear war. We've faced big problems before, but climate change is described as an existential threat; it undermines people's sense of security in a basic way."

At the time I believed we had already passed the point where the shift to a hotter world was irreversible. For years there was a consensus among climate scientists that the "tipping point," the point of no return, was when global warming exceeded 9 degrees Fahrenheit above pre-industrial levels. However, I was also aware of emerging research that suggested that it may not happen incrementally—as a steadily rising line on a graph—but in a series of lurches as various tipping points are passed. Tipping points can form a cascade, with each one triggering others, accelerating climate change. Some tipping points, the researchers said, could occur well below the 9-degree differential and may already have been breached.

After decades of trying to sound an alarm and inform the public about the threat of global warning, and being ignored or defeated, I burned out and became cynical. I was not alone. Large-scale events such as climate change and biodiversity loss cannot be addressed and fixed immediately. The result is that environmental activists often experience chronic anxiety and stress from feeling a sense of doom and gloom in face of the enormity of these global issues. Climate change is not only driving mass extinctions, ocean acidification, and an increasing number of extreme weather events and natural disasters but also taking a toll on those advocating for conservation, climate action, or environmental justice.

I didn't want to discourage their natural youthful optimism aimed at protecting the planet, but I had to be honest with them about my fears and to warn them about the possible risks of taking up the cause. I read them a quote by Jana Stanfield that Gamp emailed me shortly after I left Apalachicola: *"You cannot do all the good the world needs, but the world needs all the good that you can do."* I took what I learned from my own experience as an activist and reminded them that one person can do only so much. Being informed about the problems in our world can be incredibly overwhelming for one individual and it could make them miserable if they allowed it to. Instead, I encouraged them to recognize they are not alone and are one part of a collective movement of individuals who share their passion and purpose. I heard myself tell them that we can't make a positive impact on the world if we don't have the mental, emotional, and physical energy to do so—me, mister blow-up-the-dam-and-drown-all-the-children.

Early in the 20th century, Emile Durkheim, a pioneering sociologist, developed a concept he called "collective effervescence." It was an attempt to articulate the energy and sense of harmony people feel when they come together in a group around a shared purpose. Research has found that people laugh five times as often when they are with others as when they are alone. Apparently "peak" happiness lies mostly in collective activity. I was going to miss my little tribe, and I thought to myself that even if the world was going to hell, there was still time for me to find and enjoy a little collective effervescence.

CHAPTER 22

Shortly after moving onto the island, the executive director of the Turtle Hospital offered me a seat on their Board of Trustees. I was honored but, not ready to make any commitments, I politely declined. I didn't want to close off that opportunity altogether, and I asked to be considered if another seat opened in the future. She replied that a seat had been added specifically for me and would always be open.

Gamp was delivering my book collection in a week. I had asked her to ship them, but she insisted that delivering them herself gave her an excuse to take a much-needed break from Apalachicola. I decided to go in early on the day of her arrival and explore with the Turtle Hospital director how I might best support the hospital's mission.

I was asked to provide advice and assist the Hospital in "development." Simply put, fundraising. Being a 501(c)(3) nonprofit charitable organization, they are heavily dependent on donors for most of their income. The balance comes from government grants. The Board believed potential donors would find my celebrity as an author and environmental activist attractive. I imagined I would be shuttling to the mainland more frequently to meet and greet potential donors. It was for a worthwhile cause, and I was feeling more sociable, so I accepted the position.

To my surprise, as I was leaving the Hospital's administrative offices and heading toward my car, I saw Gamp pulling into the visitors parking area. Our plan was to meet at noon at the marina where I docked Love Me. I'd left her a message about my meeting to let her know where I would be in the event it ran long, and I wasn't at the dock when she arrived. I guessed that she got there early and decided not to wait. Thinking she might like a tour, I waited as she walked toward me. She didn't seem to see me at first, and I assumed the sun was in her eyes. As I smiled and said "hi," she smiled back and then walked on past. There was no recognition in her eyes. Thinking she was messing with me, I turned and said jokingly, "What the what, Gamp?" She stopped suddenly, spun around and studied me for a moment before saying, with a measure of shock in her voice, "Eirik? Eirik, is that you? Oh my god man, you look . . .you look . . .you look amazing! Look at you!" No one in my life had ever used anything close to an adjective like "amazing" in reference to my appearance. After cutting out alcohol, eating less, eating healthier, and swimming regularly, I knew I felt a hell of lot better but hadn't considered that I might look almost unrecognizable to Gamp and certainly not "amazing."

Momentarily stunned by her reaction, my brain finally started functioning again and I blurted out what I had always felt about Gamp's natural beauty, but never expressed, "Jesus, Gamp. Look at me? Look at you! You're just so . . . beautiful!" And with that, we both didn't know what to do next and stood a few feet apart in an awkward silence. I decided to risk a little comic relief and said, "And, you smell nice too." That worked. She laughed, gave me a big hug, said she missed having me around the Last Cast, and that we had a lot of catching up to do. As I began to show her around, she said with exaggerated earnestness, "Tell me the truth. Who are you and what have you done with the real Eirik?"

After touring the Turtle Hospital and having lunch we returned to the marina where I transferred my books from her car to the boat. We hadn't made plans other than that she would drop them off after which I'd assumed she would be going down to Key West or back up to Miami to do whatever she considered to be fun and relaxing. It hadn't crossed my mind that she might be curious about where I was living until she said, "That's it? After my driving for nearly 10 hours to personally deliver your precious books you're not even going to invite me to see your place. Oh, I get it, now that you're all buff and everything you probably have a little surfer chick shacking up with you. That's what you literary types do, right? That's okay. I get it."

I said, "No, Gamp. No surf bunnies. No shacking up. Of course, if you're not in a hurry, I would love to show you my little slice of paradise. It won't take that long, and I can have you back on shore before dark."

She then said, "Eirik, honestly, I didn't drive all this way just to deliver your books, I could have shipped them. I'd hoped that we could spend some time together without a bar in between us. I like you. I enjoy talking to you. I consider you to be a friend. I didn't make any other plans. I can find a motel, but if you have space for me at your place, would it make you uncomfortable if I stayed there for a few days?"

I'd found Gamp's no bullshit directness endearing from the moment I met her. Sharing my tiny island with a group of kids was one thing, but being alone with Gamp for a few days, who I undeniably found attractive, was another. In that moment I couldn't find any good reason to say no and said instead, "I'm sorry, I just assumed you'd want . . . to, you know, find some studly-Dudley to hook up with. If you don't mind sleeping on a lumpy mattress, of course you're welcome. But we need to scoot. I don't like being on the water after dark, and I still need to pick up some groceries. You can leave your car here."

She shook her head slowly as she walked to her car to get her things and I heard her mutter to herself, "Studly-Dudley? Oh, my god."

We docked at the island as the sun was setting. Gamp asked if I'd ever seen the flash of green that everyone talks about. She was referring to that rare phenomenon when the sun dips below the horizon and light is dispersed through the earth's atmosphere, which acts like a prism, causing a flash of green light for a few seconds. I'd seen a couple while out at sea before but hadn't witnessed one from Palaita.

I told her "No" but explained that I hadn't really been looking for it either. "Let's get everything in the house, grab a couple of chairs, and park ourselves at the end of the dock. I think we've got a few minutes before the sun goes below the horizon. If we're going to catch one, that's when it'll happen" I said. "I picked up some beer, would you like one?"

Settled in our chairs, beers in hand, Gamp offered a toast. "Here's to lying, cheating, stealing, and drinking. If you're going to lie, lie to save the life of a friend. If you're going to cheat, cheat death. If you're going to steal, steal the heart of the one you love. And, if you're going to drink, drink with friends both old and new!" With that, she held up her beer and added, "To friendship!" I responded in kind, and we clinked our bottles.

I didn't expect that we would see a flash. Conditions for that to happen must be just right. In fact, it's so elusive as to almost be mythical, like a unicorn or a pot of gold at the end of the rainbow. It was a spectacular sunset. The entire western sky was bathed in red. The island took on a surreal saffron hue as a deck of low-lying clouds reflected the sun's red and orange glow down onto the landscape. But no flash. Gamp seemed a little disappointed as we sat there in silence facing the westward sky until a bright shimmering on the darkening water turned our attention to the east where the moon was rising.

There is a scene in Pat Conroy's "The Prince of Tides" where Lila Wingo brings her children out to the end of a dock to witness the simultaneous sunset and moonrise over the South Carolina marshes. Years ago, I'd committed to memory Conroy's breathtaking description of that celestial event. The passage popped into my mind, and I recited those exquisitely crafted words for Gamp as we watched a full moon begin its ascension over the Atlantic.

> "The new gold of moon astonishing and ascendent, the depleted gold of sunset extinguishing itself in the long westward slide, it was the old dance of days in the Carolina marshes, the breathtaking death of days before the eyes of children, until the sun vanished, its final signature a ribbon of bullion strung across the tops of water oaks. The moon then rose quickly, rose like a bird from the water, from the trees, from the islands, and climbed straight up—gold, then yellow, then pale yellow, pale silver, silver-bright, then something miraculous, immaculate, and beyond silver, a color native only to southern nights."

Watching the sunset and the moon rise at the end of the dock was a common occurrence on Palaita, either alone or with my little tribe. The kids were often chatty and in a celebratory mood, making toasts to the sun, the moon, the stars, fish, turtles, you name it, they toasted it. Amused and refreshed by their youthfulness, my attention was more on them than celestial phenomena. When alone, I tended to be more reflective, my focus more inward and sober. Sitting with Gamp that night was different. Our friendship had developed easily and honestly. Primarily because of our age difference, I felt she would have no interest in me as anything other than a friend. Although I was attracted to her, *what man with a breath left in his body wouldn't be* I thought, it would be sheer folly to consider there could be anything more between us. That said, I was flattered to learn that she had no plans other than to deliver my books and hang out with me. And, she had said I looked "amazing."

Her eyes seemed unusually iridescent as she gazed upward. Maybe it was just moonlight glistening on her cornea or Conroy's words had moved her, as they always did me. A light evening breeze was caressing the island. Other than the sound of the ocean lapping gently against the shoreline and the soft rustling of palm fronds, all was quiet. It felt like an intimate moment. A wave of affection and desire moved through me. She turned toward me and spoke. I don't know what I expected her to say, but I was surprised to hear, "Wow, what a show! I'm starving! How about we have another beer while I throw something together?" While I was having feelings of intimacy, she was feeling hungry. At least I hadn't said anything stupid, but my confidence that I wouldn't was shaky. There was plenty of time for my suppressed desires to terminally mortify me.

My kitchen was tiny and equipped with minimal cookware and limited condiments. I am a fastidious housekeeper, thanks to my mother, and at least everything in the house, including the kitchen, was clean and well organized. Gamp, with nothing but salt, pepper, and olive oil, managed to prepare an extraordinary meal using a few fresh vegetables and the grouper filets we picked up on the mainland. I guess it could have tasted extraordinary because it was the first time in who knows how long since someone prepared a homecooked meal for me, but I'm certain it was because she knows what she's doing. Watching her put a meal together reminded me of when I met her the first time as she worked the bar at the Last Cast, focused and efficient. Another wave of desire moved through me. I felt my breathing change and my skin flush. *Oh, shit, what was I thinking when I agreed to having her stay over. I could have lied. I could have said that I was shacking up with a surfer chick.*

After we had eaten, she asked if I'd like to join her in a night cap on the screened porch. "I stashed a bottle of Don Julio Gonzalez tequila," she said. I hesitated to respond. "It was a gift from Clara. I know you said you've cut back on hard liquor but maybe just one shot?"

Don Julio is what Clara's dead husband, Freestone, used to drink. I wondered if she knew him. I said, "Sure, why not?" While she dug around in a duffle bag for the tequila, I went to the kitchen and got out a couple of shot glasses.

She poured the shots, lifted her glass, and said, "To Clara."

"To Clara, may she rest in peace," I added.

She took a sip and asked, "Do you know something I don't?"

"What do you mean, Gamp?"

"Do you know for certain that Clara is dead?" I told her what Goose said about the plane crash.

"I know all about that, but Clara owned two planes, and rumor has it that two planes took off and headed out over the gulf from Apalachicola that night."

"That beautiful little blue amphibious plane was hers?" I asked. "Goose said the only plane he knew of in her name was the Beechcraft."

"Yes, that's true, but I know for a fact she had the blue plane registered to a business she owns in Belize."

"I don't understand, why was it reported that just one plane took off?"

Gamp explained, "I not sure but my cousin with the police department said that he thought the blue plane had foldable wings and could be put on a trailer. He said there was speculation in the office that she hauled it to an upriver boat launch and took off from the river."

It would require some serious forethought to pull off something like that under Goose's nose. "You think she was warned about the raid on her place?" I asked

"I don't know about the AFT raid, but Freestone was so paranoid about being busted he would have had a plan. Maybe Clara followed his plan."

"Could someone else have flown the blue plane?

"Owen Coughlin could have. In fact, Clara paid for all his flight training. She wanted someone she could trust to shuttle the Beechcraft back and forth to Belize. Owen had once been a minister. Served in the military. You didn't meet him? He was living in the old Japanese farmhouse before you moved in. Stocky. Kinda looked like a boxer. Jet black hair. Wears it in a long-braided ponytail."

"Oh, that guy! I never met him. From your description, I think it may have been him I saw once bow hunting out on the river once. Goose talked about him. Something about being an arson suspect."

"That's him. Clara covered all his legal fees to help him get out of that mess."

"Goose never mentioned that," I said.

"She gave him cash. No paper trail that way, you know?"

"What would it matter if it was known that she helped him out, Gamp?"

"I don't know. That's typical of Clara, though. She often said that cash keeps it clean."

"Do you believe she's still alive?"

"Knowing Clara, I think it's a possibility. What about you, what you do believe, Eirik?"

"Well, before I heard everything you had to say, I thought she was at the bottom of the Gulf of Mexico. I don't know what in the hell to think now. I'm afraid to get my hopes up, though. You know?"

After sitting in silence and staring out into the darkness for what seemed like a long time, Gamp spoke up. "Another shot?"

"Absolutely," I said. By the time we decided we should turn in, I was under Don Julio's spell. Not drunk but composed and in a luxurious state of sedation.

The cottage has two bedrooms that are on either side of the kitchen/dining/living room area which, through a double set of French doors, opens onto a screened porch that wraps around the perimeter of the house. Each bedroom also has French doors that open to the porch. The only interior doors in the house were to the bedrooms and the bathroom, and I always kept them open to allow the ocean breeze to flow freely throughout the house. I slept in the east-facing bedroom because I like being awakened by the rising sun. The second bedroom faced west. On one occasion, when an intern wanted some privacy, she slept in the second bedroom. Others seemed to prefer putting sleeping bags on the porch if rain was in the forecast or sleeping on the pontoon boat was difficult because of too much wave action. Gamp asked if it would be okay to move the single bed in the second bedroom out to the porch. I suggested that moving the mattress out there would be less complicated than the mattress *and* the frame, and she replied with a giddy, "Perfecta mundo!"

After getting her set up on the porch, I said I was heading to bed, wished her a good night's sleep, told her to make herself at home, and reminded her she was now on Palaita Island time. She said she was going to take a shower and asked if there were any "quirky things" about the bathroom that she should know about. "Nope," I said, "Not if you don't mind a few anoles watching."

She thanked me for a wonderful afternoon and evening, hugged me, looked into my eyes for a moment and said, "Good night, Eirik. I've missed you. It feels good to be here." She then gave me a light kiss on the lips and as she turned away said, "Sweet dreams."

Did I dream? Yes, I dreamed. Sweet? No, more like a highly erotic love scene directed by

Frederico Fellini starring myself and Gamp. Did it seem real? Absolutely! Was it exciting? Hell yes! Will I write about it? Absolutely not!

A nominee for the PEN/Faulkner Award and the Pulitzer Prize, Barbara Kingsolver was intimidated by the prospect of artfully putting sex into words. In the following excerpts from a March 27, 2000, New York Times, *Writers on Writers* article titled *A Forbidden Territory Familiar to All*, she addressed the difficulty of writing about sex. She stated, "No subject is too private for good fiction if it can be made beautiful and enlightening. That may be the rub right there. Making it beautiful is no small trick. The language of coition has been stolen, or rather, I think, it has been divvied up like chips in a poker game among pornography, consumerism, and the medical profession. None of these players is concerned with aesthetics, so the linguistic chips have become unpretty by association. Vagina is fatally paired with speculum. Any word you can name for the male sex organ or its, um, movement seems to be the property of Larry Flynt. Even a perfectly serviceable word like nut, when uttered by an adult, causes paroxysms in sixth-grade boys." She concludes, "Great sex is more rare in art than in life because it's harder to do."

Amen, Barbara Kingsolver. I decided my dream was an X-rated fantasy conjured up by my brain and played out in my head, and there it will remain for me to replay as many times as I choose. I know my limitations as a writer, and I don't have the skill, or the patience, to do justice in words to those vivid middle-of-the-night scenes of titillating phantasmagoria.

As I laid awake in bed that morning, I heard Gamp moving around on the porch. I habitually left my bedroom door into the living area open and had a sightline out through the open French doors to the porch doors. The porch doors opened out to the side of the island where the dock was located. Thinking she would be ready for coffee or tea, I got out of bed and slipped on some shorts and a t-shirt. As I stood up and headed to the kitchen, wearing nothing but bikini bottoms and a towel in hand, Gamp walked into view, turned around, and was looking into the living area when she saw me standing in my bedroom doorway. She smiled, waved, and said, “Good morning, I’m going to take a dip. Want to join me?” I managed to say that I was going to have a cup of tea first and asked if she’d like that or coffee. She replied, “Coffee would be great, black please,” and headed out to the dock.

I put on a pot of water and dug out the coffee press. What gave Gamp the idea that I would be comfortable with her near nudity, I wondered. We really didn’t know each other that well and I couldn’t recall any conversation we had had in the past have that would have led her to assume that I would be. If she had asked me, I certainly would have said feel free on Palaita to be in whatever state of dress or undress she felt like; we were on a secluded subtropical island, after all. It was the presumption that it would be okay that made me wonder what she was thinking. I decided that maybe I should have my first cup of tea before I delivered her coffee to her. Seeing her bare breasted just hours after my erotic dream was seriously muddling my mind and making it difficult to think, and I needed caffeine.

When I walked out to the dock with my second cup of tea and her coffee, I remembered that she invited me to join her in a "dip." I had on a pair of cotton cargo shorts which when soaked would be heavy and too constraining. *I'll just be myself and do what I normally do and skinny dip,* I thought. *No, that would be too presumptuous.* I decided that I would ask her if she would mind if I swam nude. As I neared the dock, I could see she had already been in the water. Her bikini bottom was hung out on a bush, and she was stretched out on a towel facing down. Hearing me approach, she raised her head and said, "I hope my being naked doesn't make you uncomfortable, Eirik. I just assumed that you would be okay with it. All those kids that hung out here this summer ran around without clothes."

I walked just beyond where she was lying, sat at the end of the dock and set down the tea and coffee. All the while I was frantically searching my memory for what I had told Gamp about the interns. Gathering her towel around her as she sat up, she said, "You know, the Clan of the Turtle People." Thoroughly confused, I asked her what in the hell she was talking about. "The Clan of the Turtle People, on Instagram they call themselves the Clan of the Turtle People. They took pictures of themselves, no full-frontal, but lots of tight asses. They also posted pictures of the island and the house. None of you, though."

What kind of gram?

"Instagram. You know, the app. Where people share photos," she replied.

"App?"

"Oh, Jesus, you don't even know what an app is? You remember how you sent me a text message with pictures of this place? It's kinda like that except you can set it up so whenever you post a picture, all the friends you invited to be part of your Instagram account will see it on their accounts. It's a social media thing."

"Like Facebook?" I ventured.

"You got it!"

"I don't use Facebook, but I have friends who do. My agent was pushing me to set up a Facebook account. But look, I'd love to learn more about how it's-a-gram works, just not right now."

"It's Instagram," she said slowly and a little louder as though she thought I was hard of hearing.

"What?"

"It's Instagram, not it's a gram."

Getting exasperated, I said, “Whatever. I want to know how you were able to see pictures on the Interwebs taken by people that you've never met on my island!” She rolled her eyes when I said Interwebs.

“I did a search on Palaita. You told me your island was named Palaita. I was just curious to see if anything would come up and bada-bing, pictures of naked kids all over the place taken by someone who named their account, Clan of the Turtle People.”

“No name, just Turtle People?”

“Yep, Turtle People,” she replied.

“Can I look at the pictures? Maybe by the process of elimination I can figure out who was taking the pictures.”

“Sure. Right now?”

I hesitated to answer her then said, “No, on second thought it's doesn't matter. I don't need to know.”

“Okay, whatever. If you want me to, Eirik, I'll set up an Instagram account for you and you can follow the Turtle People, it's public.”

“Public?”

“Anybody can see it.”

"Really," I said, incredulous. My sense of privacy had just exploded, and I couldn't bear to hear anymore.

I dropped the subject, and we sipped our morning beverages for a moment in silence until she asked, "Does tequila give you intense dreams?"

Oh, Jesus, I thought to myself and replied, "Not that I've ever noticed." "You?"

"No, she said. It's just that there were some very loud sounds coming out your bedroom in the middle of the night."

"Like snoring sounds? I wake myself up snoring sometimes."

"No, more like weird moaning sounds."

"Hmmm, sorry if I woke you. I'll close my door tonight," I said, hoping to get off that subject as quickly possible.

"No, no. It crossed my mind that maybe you were having a heart attack or something. You should keep your door open."

"Do I look like I'm a heart attack waiting to happen, Gamp?" I said, feeling a little indignant.

"No, no, no! Honestly, Eirik, what it actually sounded like was someone having hot sex. Okay, I didn't want to say it, but that's what it sounded like to me." I was at a loss for words. She was looking at me as though expecting a response before she added, “I mean, it’s no big deal! Everybody has sex dreams.” With that, she stood up, secured her towel around herself, grabbed her bikini bottom, and as she walked away said, “I’m going to have another cup of coffee and put breakfast together. Fruit and yogurt okay with you?” I told her to wait and that I’d help after a short swim. “I have it under control. Take your time,” she said as she stopped and turned back toward me with a smile on her face, “I’m going to rinse off first and put on some clothes. I didn’t realize I was alone on an island with a sex maniac.” Her facial expression and her tone of voice made it obvious that she was joking, and I had to laugh. I might have even blushed.

Walking up to the front porch after my swim, I noticed that one of the double screen doors had swung open. That happens unless you pull it shut with some force. I had to constantly remind the interns to do that to keep insects out the house and Iggy who, for reasons only an Iguana would know, liked hanging out under a couch on the west side of the porch. I sometimes sat there and had dinner as I watched the sun set. Could be she had discovered bits of food on the floor on one of her forays? I hadn’t seen her since Gamp arrived and wondered if maybe she had already snuck in. As I stepped onto the porch, Gamp said breakfast was ready, and I decided I’d check on Iggy’s whereabouts later. As we sat down, Gamp looked at my feet and said, “Good lord man, you need to do something about those toes.”

After breakfast I needed to run into Marathon to pick up a few more groceries, go by the post office, and top off Love Me Tender's fuel tank. I asked Gamp if she'd like to join me, but she declined and said she wanted the full experience of being alone on a private island. I told her I'd be back by lunch and that I'd pick up something for us from the Island Fish Company, a popular waterside restaurant and tiki bar. I directed her to a printed menu in the top cabinet drawer next to the fridge and told her to pick something out while I put a few things in the boat. She said she didn't need to see a menu and to pick out anything I liked as long as it was fresh, locally caught seafood. I told her that was what made Island Fish so popular.

Sometimes I imagine there is a cell phone technology equivalent of Limbo where, based on a capricious techno god's unwritten rule, text messages and voice mail are sent to wait for judgment to be handed down determining whether they may or may not pass on to their intended destination. It's the best explanation I can come up with when my phone notifies me of their arrival hours, and in some instances days, after they were sent. One such Limbo-detained text message popped back into the real world as I docked at Marathon Key. It was from the director of the Board at the Turtle Hospital requesting my presence at an upcoming reception for an "exciting" new benefactor. It had been in Limbo for two days. Fortunately, the reception was still a couple of days off, and I decided I'd swing by the Hospital before running my errands to confirm in person that I would be attending. I could have RSVPed by phone, but "exciting" was fundraising code for very wealthy and I wanted to know more about this person. I also wanted to ask if I could bring a guest in the event Gamp was still around. I was told I was welcome to invite one guest but that the identity of the benefactor would be revealed at the reception and not before then. When I inquired as to why the secrecy, the response was that it was one of the terms of the proposed endowment.

I called in the lunch order before I left the hospital, topped off Love Me's fuel tank, picked up my mail, and arrived at Island Fish just as my order was ready to pick up. Gamp and I had lunch out on the porch where she'd set a table complete with a tablecloth, napkins, silverware, and an arrangement of palm tree fronds and small yellow flowers she gathered around Palaita. It was a pleasant surprise and a welcome relief from my dining routine, if you can even call it dining. I generally snacked on nuts and fruit and small portions of prepared food whenever I felt hungry throughout the day. Evening meals were important to Yoku, and we always set a table. Before eating we would have a moment of silence and then fold our hands as one does in prayer, slightly bow our heads, and ritualistically say "itadakimasu!" (pronounced "ee-ta-da-key-mas), which loosely translated means "I humbly receive this food." The intention was to express gratitude to whomever provided the food and prepared the meal. I impulsively folded my hands and said itadakimasu after seating myself. "Eat the what mess?" Gamp responded with a confused look on her face. I explained.

As we ate, I told Gamp about the upcoming reception and invited her to join me. She said she hoped to stay longer but would have to head back to Apalachicola before noon the next day. She explained that her partner, who was covering for her at the Last Cast, had something come up. It was the first time Gamp had said anything to me that even suggested she was in a relationship, much less a partnership.

"A business partner?" I asked.

She replied, "No, she has her own business, but we help each other out."

"So, good friends?"

"More than good friends."

"Friends with benefits?"

Gamp laughed and said, "There are definitely benefits."

"Lovers?" "Yes, we do love each other."

Gamp, who has always been nothing but direct with me, was being obtuse. I said, "What is it that you don't want me to know?"

"It's not that."

"What is it then?"

"My partner is a woman, and I don't want to put my relationship with Heather in a box, Eirik. People around town are already trying to put us in the lesbian box." Affecting a snarky tone of voice she said, "Oh, there goes that lesbian couple." I'm Gamp, she's Heather, we love each other. Anything other than that doesn't matter. It pisses me off that people are so quick to stick a label on you based on who they think you're having sex with! I'm over forty years old now, and I'm tired of worrying about what people think. I just want to be happy. I'm happy when I'm with Heather." Gamp was getting defensive.

"Whoa, whoa, whoa, I said. I'm not sure what you think I was getting at, but I'm happy for you. I wouldn't care if you were in love with a porpoise. I'm surprised, that's all. You've never even talked about being interested in anyone."

She was quiet for a moment as she studied my face. "A porpoise, really?"

"If that would make you happy, absolutely, and the porpoise, of course."

Quiet again, her eyes began to moisten and then she said, "I love you, Eirik, I think you're the sweetest man I've ever known."

It was my turn to go silent. It was the first time since losing Yoku that I'd heard anyone say that they loved me. I was moved. Gamp's sincere declaration had gone straight to my heart, and I replied, "I love you too, Gamp."

"Promise me you will visit soon, Eirik. I want Heather to meet you." I promised that I would.

As I stood up and started to clear the table, Gamp suggested I leave that for later and we go for a swim. I agreed. It was hot and humid. A swim and then a cold beer in the shade of the porch under a ceiling fan was in order. As we stood on the dock at the water's edge fully clothed, she looked at me with a questioning look. I implicitly understood what she was asking and responded by stripping off everything. With an uncharacteristic girlish giggle (there was nothing girlish about Gamp) she proceeded to do the same and on the count of three we dived into the water. In that moment I experienced feeling genuinely happy for the first time since losing Yoku. I thought maybe there was some truth in the old saying that we're never too old to feel young and recalled when I met Gamp for the first time at the Last Cast. She had chided me about having a bad attitude about aging, and I responded indignantly asking for another shot of tequila, for another round of "attitude adjustment."

I've since learned that the old cliché "you are only as old as you feel" has received some scientific backing. There is mounting evidence that positive attitudes about aging may even reduce the risk of dementia, among the most dreaded consequenccs of aging. One dementia researcher evaluated a few thousand older people—average age, 72—who were free of dementia at the start of the study and followed them for four years. The participants answered a series of questions about their beliefs about aging. The study concluded that those who expressed more positive beliefs about age were less likely to develop dementia than those who expressed more negative beliefs. In summarizing the results, the researcher noted that all too often negative attitudes about aging arise from anxiety over physical ability, appearance, loneliness, or boredom. It cited several studies of older adults who debunk these perceptions stating that older adults can, and do, live enriching and very active lives and negative perceptions about aging aren't entirely valid.

We spent the balance of the afternoon alternating between sunbathing, swimming, retreating to the porch, and drinking beer. Although older, we were unquestionably no different than the Clan of the Turtle People. Sometimes we did the same thing at the same time, and sometimes one of us was doing one thing while the other was doing something different. When we were together, we talked. Among the many questions she asked, were how I'd lost so much weight, was I seeing someone, if I ever got lonely, did I still want to sell The Essex, and was I planning to live on Palaita for the rest of my life. My questions for her included, how was the Last Cast doing, how did she and Heather meet, was there anything else besides rumors that suggested to her that Clara might still be alive, and did she know anything about the investigation into Goose's botched raid on Clara's home. I told her I attributed cutting out alcohol, eating well, and swimming to my weight loss, I wasn't seeing anyone, I felt lonely on occasion but my work with The Turtle Hospital staff and interns provided me with as much of a social life as I wanted, I was taking living on Palaita one day at a time, and I'd decided not to sell The Essex and would keep it as my Apalachicola pied-a-terre.

Responding to my questions, she said that she'd met Heather years ago at her and her now ex-husband's restaurant, The Lucky Duck in Port St. Joe. They hit it off and became especially close when Heather was going through her divorce. Regarding Clara, she said she heard a rumor from a friend in WeWa that Owen Coughlin was living in Belize and working for Clara. She added that she knew for certain that Clara was still considered to be missing and that no one had attempted to declare her dead in absentia. Other than that, her being inclined to think that Clara might be alive was based on a conversation she and Clara once had where Clara confided that she was terrified that she was going to get caught in the "crossfire" when the Feds or some Mexican cartel Freestone had screwed over, came for his ass. Clara was a survivor, she said, and she believed Clara had a plan. She had heard nothing more about Goose and the ill-fated raid. I asked if she knew anyone who would know how to contact Owen. She felt certain someone did, but that Owen's friends and family had been secretive about his whereabouts for years and imagined they still were. The big news about the Last Cast was that she had renovated the old bathroom and added a second one; put up a new, larger outdoor sign closer to the street; rebuilt the stairs down to the slip The Essex was in; had started offering some locally brewed beer on tap; renovated the old kitchen back up to the health department's standards; and had a new deck built where her patrons could sit and enjoy the view of the river and bay.

By the time the sun started to go down, mosquitoes had chased us back onto the porch where the soothing effects of friendship, sun, and sea lulled us into a long, comfortable silence. She spoke first saying, "How about I take a hot shower and then I'll put something together for dinner?"

I said, "I've got dinner covered already. Bought extra take out. It's in the fridge"

"Okay, are you going to shower?"

"Yes, after you," I said.

"Alright, I'll heat it up while you're showering," she said over her shoulder as she walked away.

When Yoku died my life was divided by a line: on one side, my same old lighter self, and on the other side, my irrevocably changed and darkened self. Since her death I've read stories about others who lost life partners without warning, and they, like me, experience sorrow and pain that they can't imagine ever ending. However, I do believe everyone is different, every relationship of every kind is different, and that there is no standard timetable for grief. Finally, I was accepting that I could never fill the void left by Yoku's death. I was also feeling confident that I was growing into a different self and into a life where I would laugh again and maybe even love again. I was lost in my thoughts and feeling a deep sense of gratitude for Gamp's friendship when she walked up behind me, put her hands on my shoulders, kissed me on the top of my head, and said, "Shower's all yours."

Over dinner we talked about Gamp's departure in the morning. The drive time from Marathon to Apalachicola is about 11 hours, not including pee stops and a lunch break. Add 30 minutes to get her to the mainland and her car and it would easily be a 12- to 13-hour day. She said she would like to shoot for being on the road by 8:00 and that if the drive got to be too much, she'd find a motel. I said I usually was up at sunrise and would have breakfast ready. She said she was an early riser too and we could prepare breakfast together. In less than 48 hours I had gone from feeling uncertain that her staying on Palaita was a good idea to not wanting her to leave. I was going to miss Gamp, but I knew we would see each other again. It was time spent with a kind, intelligent, and mature woman that made me realize how deeply I missed having a companion. Clara and I were becoming close and then she disappeared. I found myself resisting the possibility that she was still alive. I wasn't going to get my hopes up only to be disheartened again. I would have to see her with my own eyes.

As we cleared the table, I said, "Nightcap?".

She said, "Sure. Wanna another nip of that Don Juilo?"

"Does a goat stink?" I replied, channeling one of Goose's favorite southernisms.

"Is that anything like, "Is Donald Trump an asshole?"

"Precisely, I said, do you know him?"

"Oh, god no, that was one of Clara's favorite expressions, and she did know him. She said she met him through the Clintons, to whom she donated a lot of money to by the way. She may have even attended Trump and Melania's wedding at Mar-a-Lago. I know she talked about the Clintons' being invited, she said as she poured a couple of shots of tequila. Do you know him?"

"No, but I have several friends who live in New York who do. They all say the same thing, Gamp, that he's an insufferable asshole and he'd hit on a pig if you put lipstick on it. Enough about him, what shall we toast to?"

Gamp raised her glass and said, "Here's to you, Eirik, the sexiest man on Palaita."

I laughed and replied, "And here's to the most beautiful woman on Palaita." My face immediately felt flushed, but I doubted she would notice. It had grown dark, and the only source of light was two candles Gamp had placed on the porch table that were flickering in a gentle breeze coming off the ocean. Though tired, I wanted to savor the remaining time I had with Gamp. As we sat in silence and slowly sipped our tequila, I was feeling played out as I did when I was a boy at the end of one of those seemingly endless summer days at the beach. But it was getting late, and we were going to have to be up and at it before daybreak. With my last sip I placed my shot glass down and reached out over the table and offered my open hands to Gamp. She in turn finished her drink and placed her hands in mine. Tears of gratitude welled up in my eyes. There was so much I wanted to say that I appreciated about her but all I could muster was a pathetic, "Thank you! It's been such a pleasure to be with you."

Smiling broadly, she replied, "No, no, no, my friend, the pleasure has been all mine. Thank *you*!"

With that, she stood up, opened her arms wide and said, "Come here, I want to give you a big squeeze." As we held each other in a close embrace, my sense of time narrowed until all I was aware of was the warmth of her body, a light citrusy fragrance on her neck, and my heart beating.

"I said, "Good night, see you in the morning."

She said, with a wicked grin, "Sweet dreams."

I'd been dead asleep when a scream awakened me. There was silence for a moment, and I thought I may have been dreaming. Then the screaming started again. It was Gamp. I grabbed the LED "torch" I kept by my bedside. It was the same one I kept on The Essex and had way more power than I needed for use as a household flashlight. My thinking was that if I ever had an intruder it would serve to blind them long enough for me to incapacitate them or escape. I jumped out of bed, the high intensity beam of my LED blasting through my open bedroom door and scouring everything beyond, including the porch. Gamp, with panic in her voice, shouted, "Eirik, Eirik! There's a giant python in my bed" as she ran from the porch and turned toward me looking directly into the brilliant beam of light. She instantly threw up her hands to cover her eyes and yelled, "Oh my god, not that dam thing again! Turn it off!" I directed the light away from Gamp who continued to cover her eyes. I walked over to her, put my arm around her waist, and directed her to follow me. I guided her to my bedroom where she sat on the edge of the bed.

Flash blindness is caused by the oversaturation of the retinal pigment. As the pigment returns to normal, so too does sight. In daylight the eye's pupil constricts, which reduces the amount of light entering after a flash. At night, the dark-adapted pupil is wide open, so flash blindness has a greater effect and lasts longer. She had uncovered her eyes, and I suggested that she lie down and not do anything until her sight was normal again. She asked how long that might take. I told her I didn't make it a habit of blinding people and didn't know and to just relax while I went out and checked on whatever had crawled into bed with her. She replied,

"Smartass. There should be a law against people owning nuclear-powered flashguns." I picked up my regular residential flashlight off the kitchen counter and turned off the torch before going to the porch.

I was certain there were no pythons on the island, and I suspected Iggy, who was over five feet long, had crawled into bed with Gamp to get warm. Sure enough, it was Iggy. I'd never tried picking her up before, and it wasn't a good time to start. She was clearly freaked out and bobbing her head as I approached her, which is what iguanas do when threatened. They have sharp teeth and do bite people, but only in self-defense. Aside from their teeth, they have powerful tails and sharp claws. I decided to try and coax her off the porch. Iggy loved bananas, skin and all. I went to the kitchen and chopped a few into thirds. Placing one chunk close enough for her to lick, I spaced out the others starting at the edge of the bed and ending at the screen doors. I didn't want to leave the doors open and allow mosquitoes to come in, so I had to wait as she slowly ate one chunk and then another. When she finally reached the last banana chunk, I opened a door and nudged her off the porch with a broom.

I didn't know how long it had taken to get Iggy out of the house, but when I went back into my bedroom to check on Gamp, she was under the covers and appeared to be asleep. I needed to get back to sleep too, but the porch wasn't an option. Iggy, to put it delicately, had destroyed the mattress on the porch.

As I turned to go into the living room and sleep on the couch, Gamp spoke asking, “Did you get rid of the python?”

I said, “It was an iguana and it’s gone.”

“Is it safe to go back to my bed?” she asked, her voice heavy with sleep.

“It’s safe but you stay where you are. I’m going to sleep on the couch.”

“You won’t be comfortable on that couch, Eirik. I’ll sleep on the couch.” I insisted that I’d be fine. She was quiet for a while and then said, “Let’s both sleep in your bed then. It’s big and comfortable. There’s plenty of room for both of us. Come on, Eirik, come to bed.” It was true. My bed was big and comfortable, and it was where we would both have a better chance of getting a decent amount of sleep. I was exhausted. At that point I just wanted to lay down my head, and it didn’t matter where.

“Are you sure, Gamp?” I asked.

“Get in here, I’m tired of talking about it.”

As I awoke, I could see the sky was brightening. Gamp was still sound asleep, and we were already running late. It had been a rough night. I decided to let her sleep a little longer. My plan was to slip out of bed without waking her and brew a pot of coffee. However, that wasn't going to be easy. She had snuggled up to me and draped an arm across my chest, her head resting on my shoulder. I decided if I scooted my butt to the edge of the bed, I could then swing my legs out and slowly extricate myself. With the first movement of my butt, which I thought was imperceptible, she sighed and moved her arm downward across my abdomen with her hand coming to rest on my boxer shorts directly on top of my penis. Feeling the weight and warmth of her hand, I froze. The only time since Yoku's death anyone had the occasion to touch my penis was during an annual physical given by my primary care physician, a morbidly obese, 50-year-old man with bad breath in a cold, windowless, shockingly bright room. That situation could not have been any more different from the one I found myself in now.

Although virtually paralyzed by the awkwardness of the situation, there was one appendage of my anatomy that was beginning to respond to the attention it was getting from Gamp's hand. Raised Catholic in the 40s, I was taught that most anything sex-related outside of marriage was sinful which I assumed included having an erection. Consequently, going through puberty I was in a constant battle with the temptation to sin. One technique I unsuccessfully tried to deploy when having erections (which occurred for no apparent reason to me other than my heart was beating) was to petition for divine intervention and flaccidness by reciting the Lord's Prayer.

Having no regard for my plight or respect for the Lord, to my horror, my now 67-year-old penis had unilaterally decided that nothing less than a full expression of appreciation for the unexpected attention from Gamp's hand was the appropriate thing to do. Feeling mortified, I was taken completely by surprise when Gamp opened her eyes and said, "I'm okay with whatever makes you happy, Eirik," and then she gave my renegade penis a gentle squeeze.

A reviewer once claimed that Barbara Kingsolver had written the shortest sex scene in the English language. In the scene, a female character notices a cellophane crackle in a male characters shirt pocket and declares that, if he has a condom in there, this is her lucky day. Kingsolver resolves that declaration suggesting the female character was sexually attracted to male character with: "He did. It was." To Gamp's declaration that she would be okay with whatever would make me happy, I responded, "Are you talking about what I think you're talking about, Gamp?" She responded with a second squeeze and an impish smile. With that, we went about seeking happiness.

While driving Gamp to her car, which was parked at the Turtle Hospital, I asked, "What about Heather?" She told me that it was sweet of me to be concerned about her relationship with Heather but that there was nothing about it that was traditional. "What about your getting back to Apalachicola later than you planned."

She smiled and said, "I'll just tell Heather the truth—something unexpected came up." I've never been particularly good at knowing when someone is using sexual innuendo. It wasn't until Gamp stopped walking and said, "Really, you didn't catch that? Something unexpected CAME UP."

"You mean?" and I pointed to my crotch.

Laughing she said, "Yes, Eirik, I was talking about your dick! Oh, good lord, and now you're blushing. Come here and give me a hug, I really do need to get on the road."

As we wrapped our arms around each other, I said, "I love you, Gamp. Thank you for . . . *everything*. I'll stay in touch."

She said, "Aww, Eirik, I love you too. Come see me soon, promise?" I promised and told her to go ahead and find someone to give The Essex a deep cleaning. She said she would, jumped into her car, rolled down her window, blew me a kiss, and pulled out onto AIA. As I watched her drive away, I felt grateful. Above all else, my time with Gamp left me feeling desired, even at my age when our youth-obsessed culture tells us old people that we are in no way desirable. In 2014 Roger Angell of The New Yorker wrote, "Getting old is the second biggest surprise of my life, but the first by a mile, is our unceasing need for deep attachment and intimate love." He was 93 when he wrote those words. In 2014 I hadn't yet looked old age in the face and was deeply in love and attached to Yoku. I felt for Roger Angell. He was an old man, but I didn't think what he was saying had anything to do with me. What a difference a few years can make.

CHAPTER 23

After Gamp left and I returned to the island, I spent hours in the evenings sitting and thinking. Looking back, I can't say I'd been waiting for change to come or that I was intentionally building a new life. Technically speaking Yoku's death made me a single person, but for many months, in my mind, I was still half of a couple. I continued to love her in death as deeply as I had in life. Even without her I tried to maintain our bond, our commitment. Eventually my grief did start ebbing away, and I gradually stopped mourning and defining myself by my loss. I will always love her, but it was time to open myself up to the possibility of loving and being loved again. It was time to live again.

In the mornings, I sat, completely at ease, completely at rest, and enjoying the quiet and tranquility of Palaita. It was the morning of the reception for the wealthy Turtle Hospital benefactor when I heard the voice of Darth Vader say, "The dark side is calling you." It was coming from my bedroom. It was Goose. He had left a voicemail message for me sometime during the night. I always turned off my phone before going to sleep. The message was short. He said,

"You need to call me as soon as you get this message. Capisce?" I headed out to the end of the dock where I'd get the best reception. Goose picked up on the first ring and started talking before I could say anything. "Just listen, Eirik. No questions. Clara is alive and well. Had nothing to do with the bunker bombs. Squeaky clean. She's back in the country. Suing the ATF. Claiming no probable cause. No more phone calls. Keep this to yourself. I know how to find you. I'll see you soon, good buddy," and he hung up. My mind was spinning. I had so many questions, and the only person I could think of who might have answers was Gamp. I considered calling her but decided to wait until I heard from Goose again. He did tell me to "keep it to myself." But I had no idea what Goose meant when he said, "see you soon." *Maybe she's in Apalachicola,* I thought. I considered packing a bag and driving there after the reception.

Knowing nothing more than that she was alive and back in the United States was making me crazy. I wanted to see her, but then it occurred to me that she might not want to see me. Surely, she had been in touch with Gamp. Gamp knew how to reach me. Then I remembered that I had carried over my old cell number to my new phone service provider. Clara had that number. Why hadn't Clara contacted me? I finally resigned myself to the fact that I was going to have to wait for Goose. Flustered by his call, I'd lost track of time. The reception was in a couple of hours, and the director, Lilly Milkas, had requested I arrive an hour early. I needed to bath and shave, find something presentable to wear, lock up the house, and do those little things that eat up your time when preparing to leave home which, when you live on an island and travel by boat, are many.

I was fifteen minutes late as I pulled into the Turtle Hospital parking lot. They were expecting me at the front desk. I was told Ms. Milkas was on a call and to please have a seat. I felt discombobulated and was relieved that I would have some time to catch my breath and collect myself. I was turning Goose's call over and over in my mind, when Lilly walked out into the lobby. She thanked me for coming and we exchanged pleasantries as we walked back to her office. I had assumed the reason she called me in early had something to do with coordinating our approach to our potential donor. I'd done a little homework about donor relations and learned that donors can be tricky. Some want frequent updates and lots of information, while others favor a more streamlined approach. Some want to see data demonstrating a nonprofit's effectiveness; others prefer meetings that are less formal. Some prefer to be completely hands-off.

What our prospect wanted was for me to pick them up at The Harborage Marina. The Harborage is an exclusive liveaboard marina. As its name suggests, a liveaboard marina is a marina that allows owners to dock and live in their boats. Technically, there is no difference between a boat and a yacht, but most boaters refer to any boat over forty feet in length as a yacht. The forty-footers at the Harborage were on the small end of the yacht scale. Lilly added the prospect was staying onboard a Nordhavn 55 and security would direct me to it. I asked, "Why me?" She said she didn't know but assumed that it was because the person was a fan of mine.

"Maybe they want you to autograph one of your books," she speculated. It seemed odd to me, but everything had been odd about my day so far and I agreed to the request.

"Do you have a pen I can borrow, I asked, just in case?"

"Wonderful, Eirik! I'll let security know you'll be arriving in about thirty minutes." Standing, she said she needed to get downstairs and help the staff set up for the reception and wished me luck. "You can pick up a pen at the reception desk."

As I drove to The Harborage, I wondered who this supposed fan could be and why all the mystery. *What if this person wasn't a fan. What if it was someone who hated my guts, and this was a setup. Would the Turtle Hospital really go through the trouble of organizing a reception for someone they hadn't vetted? Was this mystery person a friend of someone on the Board? Why would the donor not want me to know their identity?* I was about to find out. Security cleared me to enter the marina and pointed me in the direction of slip seven. I was told the name of the yacht was Happiness. Arriving at slip seven, there was a figure on the aft deck. It was a woman. She was wearing a headscarf and was turned away from me. I couldn't see her face. I said hello to get her attention. She turned around and leaned slightly over the stern toward me. It was Clara! She calmly said, "Hey, good looking. Nice tan. I've missed you!"

Struggling to maintain my composure, I said, "Hi, gorgeous, nice boat. I've missed you too! Permission to board Happiness, Captain Butterfield?"

"If it's happiness you're seeking, permission granted, First Mate Nilsson, but first you need to remove your shoes. The decking on this boat is premier-grade Red Balau."

"My feet are ugly," I said.

"Are you wearing socks?" she asked.

"No," I said.

"I have a pair you can wear."

"You know, I should be really pissed at you," I said.

"I'm so sorry, Eirik. You have every right to be angry with me. I have a lot of explaining to do. But, I love you dearly and want nothing more than for you to get your butt on this boat right now."

"Aye, aye, captain!"

EPILOGUE

It was unimaginable to me that I would ever be able to love someone other than Yoku. I didn't "process" my loss and move on with my life. I eventually came to accept that brightness can live alongside darkness. It seems in life, when loss piles on loss, grief can work itself into daily living to the point of feeling almost ordinary. I still grieve losing Yoku, but I love Clara as much as I'm capable of loving anyone.

I don't feel my life has been restored so much as it's been reinvented. Clara and I are living together and divide our time managing her small organic banana farm in Belize and establishing an environmental education center in Apalachicola. She has abandoned her idea of unleashing concrete eating bacteria (CEB) on dams; instead, we have founded The Center for Environmental Biodiversity (CEB). The Center's mission is to educate K-12 students on the importance of biodiversity; to promote sustainability; and to encourage preservation, conservation, and restoration of ecosystems. We're constructing a project-based science education learning facility on a 20,000 acre longleaf pine preserve. Once completed, the Center will be open to the public.

I lease Palaita to the Turtle Hospital for one dollar a year. They, in turn, maintain and manage it as a vacation rental from February through December with all profits going to the hospital. The island is mine for the month of January. Iggy made the mistake of cozying up to an unsuspecting sunbathing visitor, as she did with me, and giving her a lick. To say the visitor was not appreciative would be an understatement. Iggy is now the resident pet iguana at the Turtle Hospital where she is getting excellent care and lots of bananas.

The Clan of the Turtle People is still posting images on Instagram. They text me periodically. I miss my young numb thumbs.

Clara acquired TermiGen and made Goose, who retired from ATF, the CEO. We see each other often. Gamp and Heather married. The wedding was held on the banana farm. My wedding gift to them was the Essex. We see them often too.

As Goose would put it, "We're all living in high cotton."

Made in the USA
Columbia, SC
07 March 2023

13335267R00143